"Don't tell me you've never been on a great roller coaster."

Devon couldn't imagine someone depriving themselves of the experience.

Jenny shook her head. "Never."

He'd gladly share his take on the ride. This was one woman he planned to convert. He leaned forward. Closer. Firmly into her personal space.

"It's an adrenaline rush." The kind he sought out whenever possible. "A slow build that climbs with anticipation until you can barely hold still for what's going to happen next. Then a heart-flipping moment where you feel like you're going to fall over the biggest ledge of your life and your whole nervous system goes ballistic with erratic impulses. You can't breathe. You can only scream and hold on for dear life."

Unable to resist the lure of her hazel eyes hanging on his every word, he reached out to stroke a finger down her soft cheek.

In a breathless voice she said, "Sort of like sex."

Blaze™

Dear Reader,

THE WRONG BED is a favorite ongoing miniseries from long before I started writing romance. I loved reading books with this fun and sexy premise and was thrilled when my first attempt to write my own proved to be a bestselling Harlequin Temptation novel. Now that the miniseries has moved to Harlequin Blaze, the creative options for this steamy miniseries have multiplied and it is with great pleasure that I bring you my first WRONG BED Blaze novel.

When Jenny Moore sends an e-mail containing a distinct proposition for sex to the wrong man's inbox, she finds herself undressed with a captivating stranger. A good girl would probably clear up the misunderstanding and call it a night, but Jenny has played it safe for far too long. Besides, she soon discovers she's not the only one in the mood for bedroom games.

All the fun, twice the sizzle...welcome to THE WRONG BED in Harlequin Blaze!

Happy reading,

Joanne Rock

UP ALL NIGHT
Joanne Rock

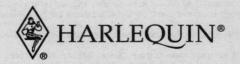

HARLEQUIN®

TORONTO • NEW YORK • LONDON
AMSTERDAM • PARIS • SYDNEY • HAMBURG
STOCKHOLM • ATHENS • TOKYO • MILAN • MADRID
PRAGUE • WARSAW • BUDAPEST • AUCKLAND

For Heather Beaufait, Amelia Hernandez and all the readers on my BlazingFans loop who encourage and support me. Thank you so much for your willingness to always talk about romance, to answer spur-of-the-moment crazy questions that help me with my works-in-progress, and for being a part of my life!

ISBN 0-373-79244-1

UP ALL NIGHT

Copyright © 2006 by Joanne Rock.

www.eHarlequin.com

Printed in U.S.A.

1

"I DON'T THINK we should see each other anymore."

Jenny Moore blinked through her first date nervousness to stare at the heartbreak hero who'd made the unexpected pronouncement. The clank of bar glasses and buzz of a hundred conversations faded in the face of her abject mortification in a back booth of an Atlantic City nightspot. Surely she'd misunderstood him.

"Our drinks haven't even made it to the table yet and you're breaking up with me?" Jenny knew she wasn't every man's fantasy date, but she'd done everything right with this executive of a Jersey engineering firm she'd met online a few weeks ago. She'd gotten to know him through an Internet dating service first. Exchanged e-mails through the private addresses supplied by the company. Tonight she'd been careful to play it cool with him even though she battled a few personal phobias about being out in public. Meeting David Brady in person was half the reason she'd come to the conference in Atlantic City—a city she'd never liked in the first place, even if she didn't suffer from

mild agoraphobia that made it tough to leave her apartment under any normal circumstances.

Today was fast becoming far from normal.

"I'm sorry, Jen, but I just don't think I can take
things as slow as you'd like me to." He gave her a
lopsided grin that might have been endearing if she
hadn't wanted to box his ears for not giving her a
chance to jump his bones—loser or not. "I just think
we need to be open and honest with each other about
our expectations, don't you?"

In an e-mail, she could have handled that question.
She'd built up a million-dollar empire selling luxury
goods online through De-Luxe, her successful brain-
child run from the isolated safety of her home office.
But now, face-to-face with a man in a situation that
made her nervous to begin with, she was more likely
to break out in hives than form an intelligent response.

"H-honesty?" Her breath caught in her throat
while she tried to ward off a bout of hyperventilation
sure to come if this man—a man who'd finally
seemed like her chance for intimacy—truly dumped
her in the retro lobby bar of Quintessence Hotel and
Casino ten minutes after their first live meet.

She'd never been a fan of dating, but this encounter was off the charts in the hideous department.

"It's not that I don't like you. I've had a great time
e-mailing with you the past few weeks." The object
of her online affection rose from the table and
snagged a pen off the nearby bar, dodging the flirta-

tious waitress who brought Jenny's drink—a pink halo—and his double shot of scotch. He passed the server a twenty with a wink and proceeded to scribble on a turquoise-colored cocktail napkin with his pilfered pen, a fat ruby winking on what looked like a university ring around his finger. "I closed my e-mail account with the dating service, but feel free to contact me at this address if De-Luxe ever gets in those platinum nameplates we talked about. Gotta be the first in town to have one for my desk."

With a quick kiss to her cheek, David grabbed his drink and sailed out of the bar, taking his khaki-clad cute butt and her only opportunity to score this weekend—maybe this whole flipping year—along with him.

Damn it.

Jenny couldn't even look at the fizzy pink halo she'd ordered when she first sat down. Her drink order had been an optimistic choice. How much more upbeat could you get than pink and fizzy? David's retreat had put her in more of a Bloody Mary mood.

"Can I get you anything else?" The busty waitress with long, dark hair peered down at Jenny's untouched cocktail once she finally yanked her gaze off of Jenny's departing date.

Thank God the server was a woman, even if the dishy chick had flirted outrageously with David when she'd taken their order. In general, Jenny did better face-to-face with strange women. Strange men were normally more intimidating. But between the online photo of David and their exchanged e-mails, she'd actually thought she had a chance of making it through a dinner with him. Possibly more.

"My friend's a doctor and he just got called away," Jenny lied in a face-saving effort, embarrassed to her toes to have a bar server feeling sorry for her. "I guess I'll just head back to my room."

Scooping up the napkin with David's e-mail address, Jenny rose from the table and headed for the elevator, her silky skirt that felt so sexy against her legs an hour ago now reminding her with each swish what a failure the night had been. She would *not* let herself contact a man who wasn't even patient enough to sit through drinks with her, so she didn't know why she clutched the stupid napkin in a death grip.

"Loser." Punching the elevator button, she told herself she would simply enjoy the conference from a self-help guru who'd written a series of books on nurturing mental help through alternative therapies that she was attending this week. She'd even been chosen to participate in a special forum with a research group compiling data on agoraphobics, so she could help along other people with issues similar to hers.

Although, it would have been nice to have indulged in some sensual therapy in addition to the mental coping strategies offered at the conference. Jenny had made an art form out of finding all her life needs online, but there were still a couple of crucial ones that couldn't be procured on the Internet.

A real relationship, for one.

Real sex for another.

Staring blankly at an ad for the hotel's boardwalk casino, she smoothed out the napkin with David's address as the elevator button chimed for her floor. He had said he was concerned about how slowly she'd wanted to take things. But surely that was a reaction to the fact that she'd confided her privacy issues with him via e-mail *before* they met in person. Maybe he'd just assumed she would want to move slowly after they met since she'd taken plenty of time to get to know him first.

And if that's what he thought, didn't she owe it to herself to clarify his mistake?

Loser or not, Dave Brady was a known quantity and Jenny wouldn't let this prime candidate for a fling slip away without exerting a little more effort. She needed a transition man while she worked her way up to a real relationship, and Dave had "temporary" written all over him.

Hot and lonesome and tired of worrying about her problems, Jenny unlocked her room and headed straight for her laptop on the king-size bed at the back of the suite. David might not be the most suave of guys, but he was a damn sight more fine than the men in her limited experience.

db@shoreengineers was about to find out how quickly she could move when it came to scratching a sexual itch.

DEVON BAINES loosened his tie as he slammed the hotel door behind him. Conferences sucked. Not because he didn't enjoy engineering. On the contrary, the workshops kicked ass and the chance to school the new kids about real-world projects was a guaranteed good time. But the bs networking which amounted to listening to a bunch of long-winded geeks sing their own praises…

Granted, he had low tolerance for people in general. An even lower tolerance for people who talked a big game and didn't have the smarts to back it up. Thank God he'd brought his laptop so he could escape the social pressures of conference hell for a few hours. Cracking open the computer, he flexed his fingers and clicked the keys that would connect him to his message box.

His watch said it was just past midnight as he slid into one of the Lucite chairs at the ultramodern wet bar just off the kitchen of his suite. Spotting the round of new e-mails, he scrolled over the mundane reminders from various project managers about in-house responsibilities and a couple of notes from friends in the industry that probably contained good luck sentiments or possible job offers. Instead, his gaze lingered on an unfamiliar address, a personal note that didn't suggest he'd won a foreign lottery or that he needed Viagra.

As if.

The note from "deluxegirl" read:

I didn't know what to say to you in the lobby bar tonight, but I came to the conference this week just to meet you in person. I'm not a woman who takes things slowly. When I see something I want, I go after it.

And I want you. Naked, hot and ready for me.

I'm in room 1016 if you're interested in seeing where things lead tonight.

Jenny

Devon stared at the note, wondering who the hell Jenny could be. An engineering colleague from another firm? Obviously, the message writer was staying here at Quintessence so it made sense she'd be connected to the business if she was here for the conference. The time on the note read 11:55 p.m., shortly before he'd left the party full of windbags downstairs. He'd been in the fifties-style lobby bar a handful of times that night, mostly because the lines were shorter there than inside the welcome reception and he'd bought drinks for some friends he hoped to do business with as a freelance consultant.

Finger hovering over the delete key, Devon tapped lightly on the button without actually pressing. He shouldn't be interested in some sordid interlude with a woman he might possibly cross paths with again in his profession.

And yet...

How long had it been since he'd lost himself in sweaty, all-night sex? For a man who appreciated every nuance of amusement park rides in his gig as a mechanical engineer, he sure did deprive himself of the best thrill on earth.

Lifting his hand away from the keyboard, he left the message intact but flipped down the screen. As if that would keep him from thinking about the mystery invitation and the potential adventure waiting one floor above him.

Suddenly thirsty, he unbuttoned his pinstriped shirt as he headed for the kitchen and poured himself a glass of water at the black marble sink with slightly gaudy—but probably pricey—gold fixtures. He didn't need this kind of temptation with his whole future career teetering on his personal reputation. But he never indulged himself, damn it. Why should he say no now when a primo opportunity landed in his lap?

Here was an open invitation that had cost him zero effort when he'd never sleep tonight anyway.

Downing the rest of the water, he buttoned his shirt back up except for the top one and left his tie on the counter. He could at least see who was behind the mystery e-mail. What would it hurt to have a look at Jenny to see if she was as tempting in person as her words had been in her note? After the last few months of having the rug pulled out from under him professionally, Devon figured he deserved to indulge a few pleasures wherever he could find them.

Picking up his room key, he stepped out into the hallway, liking this idea the longer he thought about it. His feet carried him to the luxury spa that served the hotel's suite guests where he'd seen a condom machine earlier in the day. He'd made time for a workout to sweat off three months worth of aggression toward Dave Brady, the ass-kissing nimrod who'd taken over Shore Engineers. Devon had never considered sex as an outlet for frustration, but he had to admit it sounded a lot more fun than mind-numbing reps with free weights.

Scooping up a handful of prophylactics just in case, Devon left the deserted spa and took the elevator up a floor. Straight to room number 1016.

Possibly he could have convinced himself to turn around and go back downstairs if the door had been shut. But the metal bar that served as a security bolt when latched from the inside had been swiveled on its hinge to prop the door open very subtly—a half inch at the most.

An invitation to come inside?

Lured by the implication of that open door, Devon didn't stand a chance of walking away just yet. Every primitive instinct within him urged him forward to explore his options and follow this night wherever it led. He'd been so disciplined since his ex-wife had left, determined not to let another woman mess with his head until he got his life together again.

But Lori had left…a year ago.

A damn long time to go without sex for a man with enough drive to screw his way through the phone book—according to Lori in one particularly messy argument. Not that he'd ever cheated on her. She just hated that he wanted sex a lot and to her way of thinking, he could have kept half the women in Jersey occupied with his appetite.

Shaking off bad memories and regrets, Devon told himself it wouldn't hurt to tap on the door. Body tense with anticipation even though he probably shouldn't have sex with whatever stranger waited for him inside, he knocked.

Waited.

Classical music drifted out into the hallway along with a floral scent from a burning candle he could see perched on a table to one side of the door. Beethoven and gardenias. He was pretty sure he'd properly identified the smell since he could see a face of three exotic blooms just inside the doorway.

He recognized the Beethoven from a college course he'd taken online in a futile attempt to gain refinement for his wife. He might have resented the effort except that he'd discovered he liked what he'd learned and it helped him realize Lori only liked the symphony for the social cachet. She wouldn't know Bach from Brahms if her life depended on it.

"Hello?" he called into the room, forging ahead despite multiple voices in his brain telling him he needed to back away now before he did something stupid like have sex with an uptight engineer who he'd have to sit across from in meetings some day.

"Come on in," a soft voice called from deep within the suite…another room, maybe? "I'll be out in a minute."

Devon pushed the door open wider, wondering how the scent of gardenias and the soft music could have him seriously hot so quickly. He wasn't the sex addict his ex had accused him of being. But the whole scenario of finding a titillating note on his computer in the middle of the night and then strolling into a stranger's darkened hotel room was sending strong sex signals to his brain. He'd be walking around with a serious hard-on for days if he didn't find a little relief tonight. Of course, his conscience told him to set a date with Rosy Palm and her five sisters in the shower tonight since he could not afford to mess with a total stranger.

"I'll just be right here," he called back, sticking close to the door but shutting it behind him for privacy's sake. And her safety. No woman should prop her hotel door like that.

Very reckless.

And what would a reckless woman be like in the king-size bed on the other side of the living area that was—holy crap—already sprinkled with flower petals? Pink roses, this time.

The core question that had teased the edges of his brain ever since he received the note on his computer flashed into his head in neon letters now. Lori hadn't wanted anything kinky, nothing wild and definitely no thrill rides while Devon had always liked to push things to the limit.

His skin heated as he heard a rustle on the other side of a door connecting to the living room and kitchen area where he waited. The suite was bigger than his, but the whole place was cast in shades of gray thanks to the light of three scented candles situated around the room. The one clear feature was the bank of windows overlooking the glittering Atlantic City strip and boardwalk with the ocean beyond. He took a step deeper into the suite, drawn by that rustling noise just before the door opened and revealed a half-naked woman he'd never seen before.

"Hi…" Her greeting halted in a breathless gasp, but Devon couldn't think about that since his own breath had been sucked clear out of his chest at the sight of her.

Platinum hair fell just short of her shoulders in waves that swooped over one eye. He couldn't see the color of her eyes in the glow of the candles, but then again, his male gaze couldn't remain on her face since she wore a see-through, open wrap over a white lace bra and matching panties, her generous curves showcased to mouthwatering benefit.

Garters clipped to her outfit trailed down her thighs

to hold sheer silvery white stockings in place on legs that ended in impossibly high heels. And holy hell, she was the hottest thing he'd ever seen in person or in print, and that included any beer commercial, Victoria's Secret catalog or NFL cheerleader in memory.

But as his gaze tracked back up her body with considerable effort, Devon realized the ethereal angel with the body for sin wasn't just breathing heavy for sexy effect.

The woman of his dreams was starting to hyperventilate.

2

THE HARDER Jenny tried to catch her breath, the faster it seemed to whoosh away from her in great gasping gulps. Who the hell was the guy in her room with the slightly rumpled dress shirt and no tie in sight? Had he seen her propped door and simply decided to wander in uninvited?

And where was David?

She wanted to ask the question, but no words would squeak out of a throat overtaxed with breathing. She'd never had androphobia before—fear of men—but there was a first time for everything, and judging by her vital signs, she guessed she was damn well scared right about now. Coming to Atlantic City had been too big of a risk. She should have just stayed home where none of this would have—

"Relax," the stranger ordered suddenly, his voice surprisingly calm and authoritative for a man who could be anything from a killer on the prowl to a sex fiend lured by the candles and soft music she'd been playing for her rendezvous with David.

Oh God. If she wasn't frightened before, she sure

as hell was scaring the pants off herself now. Not that she had any pants to speak of.

Her breath rushed in and out of her lungs so fast it made her dizzy. She had visions of overoxygenated blood making her light-headed. Or what if she fainted in front of this guy who could take advantage of her while she was unconscious?

Was there even such a thing as a sex fiend? God knows she'd met a few erotomaniacs at the counseling center her mother favored and they probably qualified. If the man in her room wanted something of a sexual nature from her, it sure didn't help that she was wearing only a few scraps of do-me lingerie. She'd ventured firmly into Frederick's of Hollywood terrain with this outfit. She resisted the urge to yank shut the curtains displaying the Atlantic City skyline. The last thing she needed was to turn her back on this guy and show him her thong-bared butt.

"Are you okay?" The stranger looked almost concerned for her, his straight brown eyebrows crinkling together as he studied her. "Should you sit down? Has this happened to you before?"

She couldn't catch a lungful of air to answer one of those questions let alone all three. The room started to spin and she cursed herself and all her stupid issues—real and imagined—for putting her at risk with a strange man in her hotel room.

She'd been stupid to prop the door in the first place, but she'd been afraid she'd lose her nerve to prove to David he'd been wrong about her if she didn't slip into the made-for-sex outfit. And since she would never have the guts to answer the door in a costume that was a staple in every porno queen's wardrobe, she had hoped to make a sexy entrance once David was inside instead.

"You need to relax," the man barked at her more strenuously this time as he moved closer.

The light-headedness kicked into overdrive, throwing off her balance and making her wobble on her feet, her toes curling reflexively inside the faux fur-lined white mules that her De-Luxe catalog sold as bedroom slippers. She thought for sure she would topple over and end up sprawled on the floor of her suite, but the stranger in the wrinkled dress shirt swooped in and grabbed her like some kind of super-hero before she hit the ground.

A trespassing sex fiend superhero.

Jenny figured she would have passed out then and there except that she couldn't bear to be the fainting phobic woman everyone would giggle about behind her back. Not that anyone would ever learn about this event unless the stranger turned out to be a killer and there was a write-up on her murder in tomorrow's paper, but *she* would know she'd turned into a wilting flower at the first hint of adversity and she couldn't live with that vision of herself.

The stranger's hands tightened around her waist and her bare thigh as he cradled her in his arms. At that slight shifting of his grip, the panic inside her eased by a fraction. Surely if he wanted to kill her or make free with her person, he would have done it before now when she'd been utterly defenseless.

"You're okay." He told her as if she wouldn't have the mental wherewithal to piece it together on her own. He spoke slowly. Articulating the words for exaggerated clarity.

Why bother reassuring her if he was in her room with evil designs? Some of the tension eased in her shoulders and her breathing slowed by aching degrees, her lungs burning.

Only then did she realize they were seated on her flower-covered bed. Or rather, the stranger with the straight brown eyebrows and even browner eyes was seated on the bed. For her part, she was settled across his lap, her butt dipping slightly into the depression between his legs. And holy hysteria, her hip grazed his…maleness.

Not good. Not good. Not good.

Okay, fine for him. Impressive for him. Not good for her at all.

She wriggled on instinct until the soft scrape of his light wool trousers on her thong-exposed butt made her think the better of it. This situation of a stranger on her bed holding her half-naked body close to his…impressiveness…was completely absurd and inappropriate. But duh. What did wriggling do to any man sporting that kind of condition?

The problem increased in response.

As did her shaky, shallow breaths.

"Wait." He squeezed her closer to his chest without really tightening his grip on her. Nevertheless, her breasts were a breath away from popping free of her scanty lace bra. "Sit still until you're sure you can get up without hyperventilating. You scared five years off my life and I don't even know you."

"About that…" Her voice scraped awkwardly over her vocal cords, the pitch all wrong after her bout with too much breathing.

"I'm serious, lady." He relaxed his hold again, keeping a wary gaze on her. "It's Jenny, right?"

She nodded automatically before she could consider the wisdom of confirming her identity for a man who knew more about her than most of the rest of the world between guessing her name correctly and cradling her bare thigh in his palm.

And while the sensation didn't feel *good* per se, given the fact that he could still be in her hotel room for nefarious reasons, she had to admit that having his hands on her wasn't an entirely *unpleasant* experience either. She hadn't been touched intimately since—ugh—her brief affair with a takeout delivery guy she'd slowly gotten used to seeing without leaving the safety of her home turf. But that had ended a year ago when she'd refused to go out on actual dates with him and, sweet psychosis, had she missed the sex.

"How did you know my name?" Had he been rifling through her purse while she was in her room rolling on her sexy one hundred percent silk stockings—items also available from the De-Luxe catalog?

If she hadn't been so busy trying to get David to change his mind about a relationship tonight she might have heard this stranger's entrance into her hotel suite.

"You signed the e-mail you sent me," he informed her, his hands sliding away from her body completely, silently giving her permission to walk away now if she wanted.

Except that her insides still shook and she couldn't believe her ears even though her Beethoven CD remained pleasantly soft in the background. The Ninth Symphony provided welcome familiarity in an uncomfortable situation.

"What e-mail?" She racked her brain, wondering if she'd ever met him before. Could he be with the psych conference? There were enough borderline crazy people in the Quintessence Hotel this week to ensure she ran into one every time she turned a new corner.

Sliding off his lap with as much grace as she could muster and possibly a little unwanted thrill, Jenny concentrated on taking slow, deep breaths as she kicked off her mules and tucked her legs up underneath her on the bed. The movement released the scent of roses, another sensory anchor that helped her hold steady in unfamiliar surroundings.

The sheer white robe she'd worn provided little coverage, but she drew it more tightly about her and attempted to regroup long enough to figure out what this guy was talking about. If he was an escapee from some local mental institution trying to fix himself via a weeklong psych seminar, Jenny had more reason than ever to watch her back around him.

"The note you sent inviting me to your room tonight." He stared at her as if *she* was the mental patient.

"You got a message inviting you here?" She knew he could be lying to justify letting himself into her hotel room, but she couldn't help but think about her note to David an hour ago. Could she have hit a wrong key? "What's your e-mail address?"

"D B at Shore Engineers." He straightened his shirt cuffs beneath the sleeves of his jacket. "You told me you saw me in the lobby bar earlier so I assumed you were someone attending the engineering seminar at the hotel this week. Are you in the industry? I'm pretty sure I'd remember you if we'd met before."

The tightness in her chest returned, but she forced herself to breathe slowly through the pinch. It had been almost two years since her last full-blown panic attack and she didn't plan to put herself through that scary ordeal again any time soon. She'd keep her inhalations steady now. Even.

"You work for Shore Engineers?"

That was David's firm. His e-mails had glowed with pride about the success of his company. His father's company that he'd recently taken over, in fact. How could this man have intercepted her note to him?

Unless…could David have given her someone else's address by mistake?

"I've already handed in my notice but I'm still technically with the company for a few more days." His now straight cuffs provided an interesting contrast to the front buttons of his shirt, one of which had been undone from the first moment she'd spotted him in the room tonight. He looked equal parts slick corporate guy and negligent playboy. "Are you suggesting you didn't mean to e-mail me?"

"I, um—" Wavering, she didn't wish to insult him, knowing firsthand how fragile an ego could be. But then he also deserved to understand the reason for her panic attack. "Actually, I meant to e-mail David Brady. One of your colleagues, I suspect? I thought that address belonged to him."

"This was for Wonderboy Brady?" Pointing toward her outfit, he shook his head. "Please tell me you don't know him well."

The expression of pure contempt on his face made her hesitant to tell the truth. Would she be lumped in his condescension category if he knew she'd been e-mailing David through the dating service system for the past two months? Then again, most people who weren't agoraphobic might consider that kind of contact very limited.

"I guess not." She mourned the loss of her much-anticipated sex romp now that she knew this man had received her note instead of the intended party. "*You're* DB?"

"Devon Baines. And I've been with the company longer than Brady so they let me keep the address even though I've got the same initials as the man you were hoping to contact tonight." Something about the sardonic set of his mouth told her exactly what he thought of her taste in men. "His address is Hercules at Shore Engineers, by the way, if you're still interested in salvaging a date."

Hercules?

He started to rise as if their conversation had ended. But to Jenny's way of thinking, things were just beginning to get interesting.

"Wait a minute." Either this Devon Baines was making up stories or David Brady was a far cry from the man she thought she knew. "Hercules? Are you kidding?"

"I wish I was." Cracking a grin for the first time since she'd spotted him in her room, Devon Baines gave a humorless laugh. "But in all fairness, he's had the world by the tail his first six months with the company."

"It's not like those addresses are a letter different and he could have written it down wrong or I could have read it wrong." Jenny knew she wasn't the hottest woman in the world, but she wasn't so unappealing that a man would just foist her off on another guy to get away from her. Was she? "He had to have given me your address on purpose. Is that some kind of sick joke you have going between the two of you? Write off the women you don't want by giving them phony contact information?"

Anger burned anew in her, chasing away every last vestige of fear or self-consciousness she might have had about hosting Devon Baines in her hotel room. He wasn't a killer or a sex fiend. Just a guy with a sick sense of humor. Either that, or he'd been set up.

Devon paced to the bed, retracing the steps he'd taken away from her.

"I avoid Dave Brady wherever possible, so I guarantee you he and I don't sit around concocting high school-style hijinks to perpetrate on unsuspecting women." His glare smoldered with barely leashed anger, his tall, strong frame outlined in golden candlelight giving him a glowing aura. "Jesus, Jenny, you could have called the cops when you saw a strange man in your hotel room. You think that kind of repercussion would ever be amusing to me?"

Ah, no.

Now that she heard his take on the subject she decided that wouldn't be his cup of tea at all.

"Okay." She offered up a tight smile and turned to David's other motive. "Then I guess I have no choice but to believe your coworker found me so unappealing he purposely misled me and pawned me off on a person he apparently…dislikes?" She waited for confirmation, unsure from Devon's side of the story if Dave found Devon as unlikable as Devon obviously found him.

"I can't begin to speculate why he would have given you my address and I don't know what he thinks about me personally." Shrugging, he pulled a champagne bottle out of an ice bucket Jenny had left chilling on the nightstand. "But I can't imagine any man ever finding anything unappealing about you."

He shifted his gaze from the champagne label to her and Jenny thought her skin might start to sizzle from the weight of his stare. Memories of his hands on her waist, her thighs, replayed in her mind. The heat of his touch had anchored her through her anxiety attack, helping her battle her demons more effectively than any medication.

Although there was nothing remotely medicinal about his effect on her right now.

"Thank you." She hadn't realized how starved her feminine senses were until his compliment warmed her to her toes and heated a few other things on the way. "But apparently David decided at a moment's glance that I wasn't his type. We met through a dating service online a few weeks ago, but today was the first time I saw him in person and he fled the table before our drinks arrived."

Why she felt compelled to offer the most embarrassing details of her dating history, she had no idea, but it seemed as though she owed Devon Baines some sort of explanation for his trouble. Especially since he'd gotten stuck playing doctor to her when she freaked out.

"He might be kicking butt at the office, but he obviously made a big mistake tonight." Devon settled the bottle back in the ice bucket. "And I have to tell you that if you ever invited me to crack open this highbrow vintage for you, I would never be stupid enough to leave before we kicked the bottle."

His words coaxed a smile from deep inside her despite the mixed-up craziness of her night. Her whole life.

She liked Devon Baines.

"Whether I owe the pleasure of your company to my good taste in champagne or my habit of heavy breathing on the first date, I think I might invite you to do just that since I usually never fall asleep until dawn." Another sin confessed. Since she had nothing to lose with the stranger, she might as well be upfront with him. "I'm a total insomniac."

"You're kidding." He stilled in the middle of flipping over the two slender flutes beside the bucket. "Me, too."

So he wasn't with the psych convention, but he had a few quirks of his own. Sounded like a promising start to an unexpected new…friendship?

Or more.

"Cool." Pulling herself from the bed she rose to find a real bathrobe that wasn't see-through. Something appropriate for a guy she wasn't planning to

seduce quite yet. "Then you won't think it's strange
that I love having company at 3:00 a.m. If you'll
excuse me for a minute, I'll just go find something
else to wear and we can stay up all night."

DEVON DIDN'T BOTHER resisting the urge to watch
her walk away. If this was his last view of those
thighs in garters, he'd strain his eyes for a good look
until she disappeared into the bathroom.

Well damn.

He couldn't remember the last time he'd had such
a crazy night. He'd ditched the networking opportunity offered by the seminar mixer downstairs. Then
he'd received a wayward e-mail inviting him for what
sounded like hot and heavy sex. Then the sender of
the message turned out to be a total babe who
panicked at the sight of him but offered for him to
stick around nevertheless.

A sane man would leave. Devon had a sudden
craving for champagne and a woman named Jenny.

Popping the cork on the bottle, he poured bubbling
froth into the chilled glasses on the nightstand and
told himself there was no reason in the world he
couldn't spend the night with her in her gardenia-
scented haven full of luxury if he so chose.

He got the impression she wasn't an engineer.
God, he hoped she hadn't come here for the sole
purpose of meeting Brady. The kid had disappointed
his old man at every turn, wanting nothing to do with

the company his father had built until John Brady gasped his last breath at seventy-five years old.

Devon concentrated on enjoying the moment, something he'd learned to do at a young age for a variety of reasons he didn't care to remember. And living for the moment was pretty much a cakewalk tonight when he got to share his insomnia with a woman who wore lacy white lingerie and seemed to embrace risk-taking as much as him.

"So I never told you my last name." She reappeared suddenly, a man's black and red flannel bathrobe covering her from midcalf to neck, although her feet remained covered by the sheer white silk that could only be the gartered stockings she'd been wearing earlier. An enticing prospect to know what waited beneath the flannel. "It's Moore."

"Nice to meet you, Jenny Moore." He held out a glass of champagne to her and raised his own with the other hand. "Here's to shared insomnia."

"Cheers." Accepting the glass, she clinked it against his before taking a sip. "I'm not usually the kind of woman who propositions men she hardly knows, but I've been pushing myself to take more risks lately. Be a little more bold."

Seemed to him she was doing just fine in the bold department. Her note had been…intriguingly forthright.

"Are you in town for the engineering conference?" He followed her toward the sofa away from the bed.

A damn shame she wasn't thinking about jumping his bones the way he wanted to jump hers, but he found himself intrigued by more than her silk stockings. Even wrapped up in flannel, he wanted to get to know her.

"If you knew me better you'd realize that's like asking Shaquille O'Neal if he's in town for the knitting classes." Dropping onto the white leather couch that was more comfortable than his black and Lucite-crammed suite, Jenny sipped her drink and folded her legs underneath her. "I'm a small business owner and I run a catalog company called De-Luxe. My refined tastes and love of shopping have finally parlayed themselves into a lucrative career after years of simply running me into credit card debt. I'm thinking about expanding this year and taking the company public."

"So the fur-lined slippers and the exotic vintage champagne are par for the course for you." He didn't know what he thought about that since he'd never been a connoisseur of anything beyond beer and tractors. Not that he was Joe Farmer, but he'd gotten his first taste for mechanical engineering when he'd taken apart a neighbor's old John Deere and put it together again.

"They're not real fur, just a top-of-the-line facsimile." She set her glass on the coffee table and studied him in the candlelight, her eyes clearly a shade of hazel now that he saw them up close. "And the luxury goods definitely aren't the norm for me anymore since I've learned to put most of my earnings back into the business, but there are a few items we carry that I can't help but scoop up."

"You live in Jersey?" He noticed her hands were bare of rings, her nails neatly polished in a shiny clear finish with the tips painted extra white. "You don't sound like a native."

"It took years of practice to erase the accent, believe me." She winked and he wanted to pull her closer to sit her on his lap again. "But since I started out as the sole operator for the De-Luxe 800 number, I wanted to sound a little more upscale than the Jersey twang suggests. I grew up just south of Seaside Heights, about an hour north of Atlantic City. You?"

"I started out in Philly and I still have a place there. But I keep an apartment near Wildwood since Shore Engineers is based down there. We do work all over the eastern seaboard." He'd embraced the traveling as part of his job since he still tended to go stir-crazy if he stayed in one place for too long. "In fact, I think I put in a small coaster at an amusement park just north of Seaside Heights. One of my first."

"You build roller coasters?" Her eyes lit up, brighter than the lights on the glittering boardwalk outlined behind her.

He really liked Jenny.

"I've designed a few. That's the payoff for being a math nerd all through high school. Eventually you recoup a certain amount of cool that you never could cultivate by busting the grading curve on every test." Not that Devon had ever needed anyone else's approval.

"So what's it like to create a thrill ride? Are you the first to try it out? Do you ever get scared you forgot a safety feature and you'll be tossed out of the car on your ear?" She focused solely on him, her pupils wide in the dim light.

A damn heady experience to be on the receiving end of that focus.

"I'm not always the primary tester, but I try to be whenever possible." What was the point of designing and strategizing for the best adrenaline buzz if you couldn't critique it afterward and learn from the experience? Good mechanics were all about subtle adjustments. The esoteric changes that couldn't always be accounted for on paper. "And I would consider the ride a failure if there wasn't a hint of fear along with the fun. That's what initiates the adrenaline rush necessary for a good experience."

"Really?" She seemed to contemplate that as if he'd unveiled some important secret. "You scare yourself on purpose. But don't you eventually not fear it anymore? If you take the ride too often, do you grow kind of blasé about the whole thing?"

"Not me." He'd never let that happen. "I live in the moment and actively seek the thrill. I think you can only grow detached like that if you want to take the fun out of it."

Frowning, she twisted her finger around the dangling belt of her robe. "Or if you want to take away the fear. But what does it feel like?"

"What does what feel like? Designing a coaster?"

"No. Experiencing it firsthand."

"Don't tell me you've never been on a roller coaster." He couldn't imagine someone depriving themselves of the experience.

"Never."

He smacked his forehead in disbelief, but he'd gladly share his take on it. This was one woman he planned to convert.

Setting his glass beside hers on the coffee table, he leaned forward. Closer. Firmly into Jenny Moore's personal space.

"It's an adrenaline rush." The kind of experience he sought out whenever possible, just for kicks. "A slow build that climbs with anticipation until you can barely hold still for what's going to happen next. Then a heart-flipping moment where you feel like you're going to fall over the biggest ledge of your life and your whole nervous system goes ballistic with erratic impulses. You can't breathe. You can only scream your brains out and hold on for dear life."

Unable to resist the lure of her hazel eyes hanging on his every word, he reached out to stroke a finger down the side of her soft cheek.

"Sort of like sex."

3

"MY EXPERIENCES must be lacking because I can't ever recall sex having such a profound effect." She knew she'd been seriously deprived when it came to *quantity* of intimate encounters, but now she had to consider that she'd never even enjoyed much *quality* in that department. "And since I have built a whole company around the idea of indulging your inner hedonist, I think I'm going to have to investigate this sex-as-thrill premise."

His hand cupped her chin tilting her face toward his in a way that sent her pulse into overdrive.

"It can be risky to seek adventure with someone you don't know much about."

As if she didn't have enough phobias without him resorting to scare tactics.

"Trying to warn me away?"

"Not from me." His thumb dragged slowly along her bottom lip. "Selfishly, maybe I'm just hoping you don't consider propositioning anyone else. I'd like to be the one to get to know you better."

The heat that had been flowing through her veins

cooled slightly at the reminder that her night had started off with another man.

"I'll keep that in mind if ever I feel the need to issue a proposition again." She smoothed the heavy red flannel of her robe over her knee. "Considering my first attempt landed a total stranger in my room, caused a panic attack and proved that the one guy I tried propositioning is flat-out deceitful, I probably won't put myself out on a limb for sex again anytime too soon."

"I shouldn't have brought it up." Devon leaned back on the couch, giving her enough space to start thinking with her mind again instead of her overheated body that still remembered the feel of his hands on her naked thigh. "There's a chance this guy Brady used some semi-shady tactics to squeeze me out of a job, and while I've got plenty of career doors open to me, I can't help but resent that his maneuvering flew in the face of his old man's wishes just a few months after the guy kicked the bucket. I'll admit, I might just be choking on a couple of sour grapes. But in case I'm not, you might want to be careful."

"I make it a habit not to let somebody close to me again if they hurt me once." She had enough problems with trust without putting herself on the line that way. "What about you? Are you leaving the company because this guy stole your spot?"

"I'm not willing to play games to win back the job without the board's endorsement. I probably should have made more noise about my qualifications sooner in the decision process, but I tend to get wrapped up in projects more than politics."

"So you bow out gracefully even though you don't have much faith in the company's new director?" Jenny knew she'd never have the heart to play those kinds of games either, but Devon built thrill rides for the fun.

No doubt he could successfully handle corporate politics.

"The board chose him, so maybe he has strengths I don't know about. There comes a time when peace is more important than fighting for what I might think is fair." He almost looked convinced of it. Almost. "Besides, no one promises life will be fair. You know that going in."

"So you're leaving Shore Engineers to do what?"

"Go out on my own. Do some consulting work for a few amusement parks to put together the kinds of rides thrill seekers want." He pulled over the champagne bucket and refilled their glasses. "Now that our day-to-day lives are so insulated from physical danger, theme parks are more popular than ever because they provide the edge-of-your-seat experience absent from our lives."

"I see you've given this idea of incorporating excitement into life a lot of thought." She sipped her champagne and let the bubbles tickle her lip. The dry bite of the drink made her all the more thirsty somehow, but she knew drinking more wouldn't help.

A taste of Devon Baines, however, might just do the trick.

"I grew up with an appreciation for adventure." His arm sprawled along the back of the sofa while he soaked up the view of Atlantic City and the ocean out the window and she soaked up the view of him.

How might her life be different if she allowed herself to dive headfirst into adventure sometimes instead of retreating behind the safe four walls of her apartment? She'd taken a risk and faced danger by coming here this week and look at how she'd thrived in spite of the potential consequences. She'd survived an anxiety attack and met a fascinating man in the process. Her agoraphobia didn't have to rule her life.

It had robbed enough from her already.

"I think a man with so much experience in adventure would make a very good guide in the realm of thrill-seeking sex."

God knows where she got the nerve to say it. Maybe it had been the champagne talking, although with only a small glass and a bonus sip to her credit, she hardly thought so. And damn it, she stood firmly behind the sentiment. This was her week for adventure.

Devon stared out the window at the sparkling lights below for so long she wondered if he'd heard her. But then, he turned the full, heated impact of his gaze toward her and she knew he'd most definitely heard.

"Are you in the market for a guide, Jenny?"

His low-spoken words seemed to tremble through

her skin, reverberating along her nerves and stirring her very blood. She would never find another opportunity like this, a stranger who came to her—on safe terrain—in the middle of the night and stayed with her until she wasn't scared.

Until she was entirely intrigued.

"Yes I am." She didn't hesitate. "I want the thrills."

Devon had never heard sweeter words. A plea for sex from a sensuous woman who wanted as much adrenaline in her ride as he did.

He reached for her the same moment she leaned toward him. Fingers sinking into the chin-skimming platinum hair, he hauled her close. Her gardenia scent teased his nose for a moment before his mouth found hers. He drew on her lips, tugging the lower one into his mouth to nip and suck and taste her. Her champagne flavor and slick warmth made his senses spin and he reached to pull her back on his lap where he'd wanted her to be again ever since he'd held her there earlier.

Jenny wound her arms around his neck, and then, too restless to be still, she trailed light scratches down his back, hastening him. He'd never expected this woman, garbed in delicate white who'd hyperventilated over the sight of him in her room, to generate so much heat.

The music playing had switched from Beethoven to Rachmaninoff, a venture to the dark side that suited Devon's mood well. Tunneling beneath her flannel robe, he cupped the smooth curve of her sweet, heart-shaped ass that he hadn't gotten to appreciate nearly enough the first time she'd been seated across his thighs. She wore a lace and satin thong cut in a mouth-watering V shape as if to point him in the direction he needed to touch. As if he needed any reminders.

But he couldn't go there first, not when he'd promised a thrill ride she wouldn't forget. First they needed the slow, upward climb, the steady build of anticipation that made the first plunge knock your breath right out of your lungs.

Careful not to stray beneath the elastic of her panties, he skimmed his palm up over the curve of her waist to cup one lace-covered breast. The weight in his hand had him even harder than he'd been five seconds ago, which was saying a hell of a lot since he didn't know how much more a zipper could take.

Thankfully, her restless fingers tracked down his shoulders and over his abs to address the situation, although the way she brushed and grazed the head of him as she worked threatened to take him over the first precipice too damn soon.

Covering her fingers with his own, he helped her ease down the zipper. "I'm not going to be much of a guide if I lose it before we get naked."

"Are you kidding?" She didn't even pause to look at him in her fascination with what she'd unveiled. "We could stop now and this would still be the biggest thrill of my life. The very biggest."

She peered up at him then through her lashes, a

slow smile of invitation curving her swollen lips. The subtle suggestion that she would comply with just about anything he wanted held him riveted.

And just like that his control started splintering. Sex with Jenny wouldn't be about finely tuned mechanics and seamless engineering. Things were going to get wild and out of his control and there wasn't a thing he could do to change that.

He peeled away her robe, tugging the tie free until the flannel fell from her shoulders and slid to the floor. Her bra strap drooped down her arm along with it, and Devon peeled the cup the rest of the way off to expose first one breast and then the other.

She was so pretty, her creamy skin pale and perfect and highlighted by taut, rosy tips that puckered even tighter as he watched. He bent for a taste and her spine arched, head falling back as he licked, suckled and drew on each pebbled nipple. His hands worked the clasp as he laved the delicate skin, freeing the soft cleavage for him to gently knead and squeeze until she moaned and writhed beneath him.

Her leg snaked around his hip, telling him exactly what she wanted. He wanted that, too. Wanted *her.* All over him.

She was so soft. Her hair. Her breasts. Her silky skin. And that utter femininity, the distinct sexuality of her body, made him rock-hard by contrast. He edged her backward on the sofa, leaning her down until her shoulders hit the leather cushions. The need to be on top of her, over her, dominating her at least this first time gripped him with a fierceness he didn't recognize.

"This time will be fast." But he wasn't leaving until he'd given her everything, until he couldn't remember his own name. "And hard."

"I'm ready." She undid the buttons on his shirt, shoving away the starched cotton to feel his skin. "More than ready for that."

Lifting off her enough to step out of his clothes, he heard a champagne glass roll across the coffee table and thud to the carpet on the other side. A candle flame somewhere in the room wavered wildly from the air disturbed by tossing his clothes away.

"Are you sure?" He pulled her thong down her thigh, blessing her foresight for wearing the panties over top of the lace garter belt hugging her waist. "Because I need you really ready for me. Hot. Wet."

He kissed her mouth as his hand parted her thighs to see for himself. And she was both. So damn hot. Wet enough to slick his finger with her and tease a shudder from the touch.

"You like that, Jenny?" He would gladly stroke her this way all night if he could make her quiver again.

Her hazel eyes fluttered open to stare up at him in the warm glow of candlelight, her pupils dilated so wide he could scarcely see the irises.

"I'd like more," she whispered, her tone full of spark and fire even when he had her trembling beneath him. "I want all of you inside me."

Ah damn, now it was him who suppressed a shiver, her words teasing him more powerfully than any touch.

"Condom." Why hadn't he taken the ones he'd grabbed at the spa out of his pocket before he tossed aside his pants? "Wait."

He reached for his trousers, hands practically shaking with the need to have her now. It had been so damn long for him and being with Jenny was like a libido accelerator, propelling him forward on raw sexual need.

"Let me." She checked the other pocket while his hand tangled in the first and a second later she emerged with a foil wrapper. "I want to put it on."

He grit his teeth, knowing he'd never survive her hands on him but damn it, he couldn't say no when this time would be so quick.

"Okay." His voice hit a ragged note as he tossed aside the couch pillows to make more room. "But I'm hanging by a thread here, Jen."

He watched her face while she worked, unable to enjoy the visual of her hands on him or he'd be done for sure. To her credit, she rolled it on smoothly, quickly.

"Me, too," she whispered back, spreading her legs for him to take his place between them. "I need you so—" her voice caught as he eased inside, the room going silent for a long moment before he thrust in the rest of the way and she squealed in response "—badly."

He held her steady to kiss her, lick her, devour her.

He needed to get used to her, to halt the rapid-fire hammering of his pulse so he could give her the ride she deserved. Somehow, some way, he'd scavenge up at least that much control.

"Oh. *Ooh.*" But then her breathless sighs started, her sweet moans and soft cries that were better music than anything Rachmaninoff could have created.

Devon lifted her enough to swivel her body, planting his feet on the floor and seating her on the couch to give himself leverage. If good sex owed anything to mechanics, he'd get this right for her. Control or no control, damn it.

Slipping two fingers between their bodies he found her clit and circled. Her thighs tightened and he picked up speed as he moved inside her, the couch cushions sliding beneath them as he thrust.

Her cries increased as his fingers worked, the broken words panting, chanting in his ear.

"Please, please, please. Yes, right there."

He could feel the throbbing of her feminine muscles, the clamping and unclamping until she squeezed him so damn tight he couldn't hold back another second.

"Ooh!" Her shout of satisfaction mingled with his own, their voices ragged and rough while their bodies hummed and vibrated together in one last straining dance.

Jenny's breathing slowed and finally evened out, but Devon didn't think he could move. Not quite yet anyway. Their bodies remained sealed together by sweat and sex, skin sticking to the leather sofa. He just lay slumped over her, replete, and listened to her breathe while the sounds of a ruckus in the suite next door floated through the wall. Not a ruckus exactly, just some headboard banging that made the pictures—all framed views of Atlantic City—vibrate against the wall.

Jenny didn't seem to notice or chose to ignore the slight racket as she smiled up at him, the candle glow reflected in her eyes.

"That was quite a ride." Her mussed hair only made her look sexier, like a wanton angel come to tempt him. "No wonder you love your job."

IN THE SUITE next door, David Brady rode the petite brunette he'd chosen for tonight's fun and found himself frustratingly distracted by thoughts of the little Miss Innocent he'd had drinks with earlier that night.

Jenny.

He didn't usually like blondes, especially the naive variety, so he'd been all too happy to pass up on her charms in favor of someone more experienced.

Like Sasha, here.

"Oh please, don't hurt me," she cried out in mock fear over the noise of the black lacquer headboard rapping the wall behind it, her panting breaths coming even faster than his lightning-quick thrusts. "I'm so sorry I was a naughty girl."

David knew Sasha the cocktail waitress wasn't one bit sorry since she'd come twice already while she talked herself into a frenzy. He peered down at her upturned cheeks as he plowed into her from behind and wondered how to get the blonde out of his head long enough to enjoy his time with the saucy server who'd fondled him under the table tonight when Jenny had gotten up to powder her nose before their drinks arrived.

Really, how could he expect a novice like the De-Luxe proprietor to compete with the waitress who'd gotten inside his zipper in two seconds flat, all without anyone realizing what she was up to?

And yet...

Something about Jenny Moore had called to him. She obviously liked him more than he'd realized since there'd been a moment she looked totally dis-traught once he excused himself from their date. And that adoration appealed to him. Had he been too hasty in choosing the quick payoff over a woman that might have been more intriguing in the long run?

"Oh yes!" Sasha shouted, spreading herself wider for him, all while shifting his hand to her bottom and making not-so-veiled references to her need to be disciplined.

How did he end up with all the S and M junkies lately?

Not wanting to disappoint her, he trotted out a few stock "bad girl" phrases to keep her in the mood, his brain miles away from the sex that left him rock-hard even after two hours of antics with his energetic bed partner. He prided himself on being a skilled lover, enjoying the thrill that came with giving a woman everything she wanted until all she saw was *him*.

But tonight, for some reason, that wasn't enough.

Maybe it was time for him to challenge his sexual prowess. Test his powers of seduction. Women like Sasha were so easy to please. There wasn't the thrill of the chase the way there would be by courting an innocent like Jenny.

How would he strategize her seduction? She had some phobias. Fears.

Rolling Sasha to her side for a better angle, David thought maybe he could overcome Jenny's fear of strange places by taking her someplace safe. Secluded. She'd feel more comfortable if she could simply concentrate on getting to know him. And he could discover all her sexual secrets, all the things that made her unravel.

Already the idea teased his imagination, tempted him out of this evening's ennui so that he could enjoy the feel of Sasha around him.

Did it really matter that he had to envision Sasha as an innocent blonde instead of a sizzling, knowing brunette? The firebrand waitress would never know the difference. She was too busy staving off another orgasm.

Seizing any idea that would salvage the night for

him, David reached for his discarded tie tangled up in the bed linens.

"Bad girls need discipline," he reminded Sasha, sliding the silk around her eyes and knotting the ends behind her head. "I think you're going to have to work a little harder to please me after the way you sent my date running tonight."

"Very naughty of me, wasn't it?" Sasha smiled. He could tell from the way the blindfold lifted on her ears, her cheekbones shifting with the movement.

She was sassy and full of herself, and David promised himself to give her everything she asked for and more. Right after he finished his daydream about satisfying Jenny Moore beyond her wildest dreams.

He needed an innocent in his life now that he'd finally found his rightful acceptance in his father's world. And Jenny was a woman he could trust not to embarrass him at corporate functions and feel up his coworkers under the table when he wasn't looking.

He couldn't bring women like Sasha around Shore Engineers, not with know-it-all engineers like Devon Baines ready to steal away everything he'd worked so hard for since his father died. The thought of Devon, the protégé David's father had fawned all over when he turned his back on David, made him thrust into Sasha a bit harder than he'd intended.

But she liked those kinds of games anyway, right? She'd forgive him.

His seed spilling in her tight passage, David

shouted his fulfillment, but even that didn't bring him as much pleasure as he'd hoped since the name on his lips wasn't the sweaty waitress who had practically begged him to take her to his room. It was Jenny Moore with all the irrational fears and issues they'd talked about online for two months. He should have never given her over to Baines, thinking she'd annoy someone who prided himself on having his life so perfectly ordered.

No, David should have realized the sweet intensity a softer female could bring to his bed.

His cock bobbed responsively at the thought while Sasha recovered from their third go-round in the sack. Had she come that last time? He hated that he didn't even know. But he was too busy dreaming up plans for winning back the woman who could help him secure his future as head of his father's company despite the selfish old man's wishes.

4

JENNY MOORE—Manhunter Extraordinaire.

She smiled to herself as she watched Devon move about the hotel room, picking up champagne glasses and straightening a couple pieces of furniture gone slightly askew in their frenzied need for one another. How delicious that he felt the need for order, this wild man who'd just spoiled her for sex with any other male. Gotta love that engineer attention to detail, especially when the details included every inch of her body.

Except that she wouldn't *love* this man. She would simply pleasure herself—and him—with this red-hot chemistry they'd discovered until they were both too exhausted to move. And that's what qualified her as a masterful manhunter. Even if she'd found this particular man by accident.

She'd still walked away with a blue-ribbon stud.

"You look pretty damn pleased with yourself, Ms. Moore," he remarked as he scooped up their clothes and draped them over the back of the couch. "Are you thinking about what a sucker I am for garters?"

"I was thinking how good you look naked." She'd never had a man in her life for long on an intimate level, and her couple of trial runs with guys who were more friends than lovers had been less than inspiring. So seeing vitally attractive Devon prowling around her suite was a luxurious treat foreign to the De-Luxe CEO, even though she was normally an expert on pleasure seeking.

What fascinated her now was the obvious interest he—all of him—paid to her compliment.

"You're making it tough for me to give you any recovery time with that kind of talk." He paused in his straightening long enough to check out the CDs she'd brought along. Pressing the random option, he stalked toward her as a Strauss selection hummed through the speakers.

"Who needs recovering?" Staring at him was giving her hot flashes, her whole body clamoring for more. "Tonight is a one-time indulgence for me so I've got to make the most of every second."

"One-time?" Frowning, he stretched out over the bed, completely invading her personal space in an unmistakable message as he covered her. "Are you going back home tomorrow?"

"No." Her breath caught in her throat to feel him on top of her, even with a sheet and a thin blanket in between them since she'd burrowed under the covers, less confident in her naked body than he seemed to be in his. Although judging by the way he'd touched and kissed her, maybe she didn't have any reason to worry. "I'm here all week."

She hoped he wouldn't ask her the specifics about her reasons for staying in town. Baring her body had been enough of a step for her tonight without baring her soul, too. She didn't know what he'd think of her agoraphobia, this man who lived for the next thrill. But she would rather not risk their heated connection with the mundane details of real life just yet.

"You're here all week and you're limiting this to a night?" He bent to swirl his tongue in the hollow at the base of her throat. "I obviously didn't do my job before if you can turn your back on us so fast."

She swore she could feel the effects of his tongue the whole length of her body. Tremors of pleasure skimmed all over her skin as he slid under the blankets with her.

"Hey, what is this?" He paused to peer down at the hot pink bed sheets, then run an appreciative hand over the silky smooth finish.

"Egyptian cotton. Insanely high thread count." She loved these sheets and had sent them ahead to the hotel to ensure her comfort and peace of mind.

And because the only way she could travel was to bring snippets of home with her to give her brain familiar things to focus on, like her music.

"You treat yourself well, don't you? The gardenias, the candles, the sheets—none of it feels like a hotel room to me."

"Some of us find our thrills closer to home." Flipping back the sheet, she showed him the cashmere blanket she'd brought in her suitcase. Okay, her trunk. When you traveled with big issues and even bigger blankets, your bags tended to be on the large side.

"I'll be damned." He ran a palm over the soft blanket and his gaze narrowed. "You're a hedonist."

"Guilty." Better he think that than know the whole truth. Besides, she *did* like to indulge herself.

Releasing the blanket, he straightened the sheets again and pulled her close. "Do you have any room in your life for things that aren't all soft and smooth?"

He was ramrod hard against her, the heat of his skin practically singeing her.

"That can be pleasurable, too." Her voice was whisper thin, her whole body molding around his, heat pooling between her legs.

He drew the sheets up over their heads, sealing out the world and consigning them to a hot pink tent. Good thing she wasn't claustrophobic or she'd be sprinting for the door. But the close quarters actually soothed her, narrowing the big, bad world down to just the two of them. The sound of their ragged breathing intensified in the muffled quiet, the music from the CD fading inside their refuge.

"I'm going to change your mind about one night," he warned her, his head ducking to her neck where he kissed his way down her throat. "Tonight we can stay close to home, but before the week is out I'm going to take you down to the Steel Pier. There might not be a roller coaster, but maybe we can convince someone to crank up the Ferris wheel and stop us right at the top."

Her heart paused for a two-count and then picked up speed at the thought.

"You wouldn't be so wicked." She'd have to psych herself up for days just to get back in her car for the drive home. The Steel Pier on a crowded Atlantic City boardwalk was out of the question for someone with her mental disposition.

"In the name of making your heart beat faster," he traced his fingers over her right breast, "just like it is now, I'll be as wicked as I please."

She knew he'd probably run before then, as soon as he found out about her very large emotional baggage, but she couldn't help savoring the idea of a risk she'd never take. Just because she wasn't brave enough to put herself out there in new and potentially scary situations didn't mean she didn't dream about them. Fantasize that she could take chances and live on the edge the way Devon Baines did.

For now, that was enough.

She sank her fingers into his dark hair to steer his kisses lower. As long as they were playing games of self-indulgence and wickedness, she would show him exactly what she wanted.

His heated kisses had made her breasts ache for

direct contact. When his mouth found her, nipping, licking, she threw her head back with the pleasure of it. She undulated beneath him, seeking the best angle, the most heat and pressure from his lips. But the more she satisfied the ache in her breasts, the greater the unrest building between her thighs. She craved his touch, and even more she craved his kiss.

There.

But she was not ready to be that wicked. Not yet. Perhaps if she demonstrated her want by example, tasting him the intimate way she wished to be tasted...

She explored his body with shaking fingers, her nervous system overloaded with sensory impulses and overwhelmed by sex. Devon's back narrowed into his waist, rippled with unexpected male muscles along the way. His obvious strength surprised her for a man she imagined must work behind a desk with computers and— She didn't begin to know *what* engineers worked with.

"I want to touch you." She breathed her request into their haven, the sheets cloaking them in silky luxury.

"The feeling is mutual." He licked a kiss into the dip of her navel and she flinched with the erotic feel of his tongue there. Swirling. Teasing.

A bolt of desire flashed white-hot to her core and she could almost imagine what it would feel like to receive his kiss right where she needed him most.

"But I want—" How to say it? Words evaporated from her head as he nipped a soft bite along her abs.

"I think I know what you want." His dark promise sent her eyelids fluttering as she gave herself over to whatever he wanted to do.

He seemed so damn sure of himself, so much more at ease with the intimacy than she'd ever been, she figured it wouldn't hurt to simply close her eyes and hang on tight. That's what one did with the best rides, right?

And then he shifted lower still, his hands sliding beneath her thighs to spread her legs. When he huffed a breath of sultry warm air over her mound, she thought she'd fly apart then and there. The deep intimacy of the act combined with the fact that she'd completely exposed herself to him, sent tremors through her limbs.

Not unlike the moments before she hyperventilated.

In fact, her breathing grew quick and shallow as he slid his tongue along the seam of her, a pleasure so dizzying she thought she'd faint from it. He growled his affirmation, a primal, guttural sound that pulsed through her most delicate parts. The vibrations hummed inside her, heightening the sensation of his kiss and making her feminine muscles clench in response.

The heat beneath the sheets soaked them in sultry sweat. Jenny clutched handfuls of the linens, trying to anchor herself against the waves of pleasure quickly building up inside her. She wanted to savor the exquisite feel of his mouth on her, but the coiling tension tightened too fast.

When he swirled his tongue there, the way he had done to her navel, she gasped at the raw sexuality of it. Dark. Blossoming. Seemingly endless in its power to undo her. She came with a fierceness she'd never experienced, the vitality and passion of this one orgasm rocking her from her toes to her hair follicles, leaving no cell untouched, consuming her very being with one lush contraction after another.

And Devon drove her onward, his mouth giving her no quarter, tongue delving still deeper to tease another release hard on the heels of the first, as if he would never let her go from this fluid, delicious moment of passion.

Her legs gripped his shoulders, her muscles so taut and tense she wasn't sure she could release him if she wanted. But then the last tide of sensation seemed to sweep through her and her thighs relaxed, falling away as he moved up and over her.

He crinkled a packet.

A condom?

She hoped so. She thought so. But then, of course a man who straightened wrinkled clothing would remember protection. And something about that tiny hint of neuroticism in him made her smile as she drew him up over her, needing his weight on her, the feel of him in her arms.

"You can touch me next time." He sounded almost apologetic, as if he'd neglected one of her wishes, and Jenny promised herself she would find time to repay him in spades for showing her what a mouth-induced orgasm felt like.

Damned if it wasn't one luxury no woman should do without.

"I'll hold you to that." She twined her arms around his neck. "Right now, I just need you inside me."

He obliged slowly, as if he understood it had been a long time for her since she'd had sex twice in one night, although actually twice was a new record for her. But even with the slight soreness, the ache for him was a greater concern.

He gripped her jaw with gentle fingers once he was all the way seated inside her.

"Don't hold anything back, Jenny." His eyes darkened, a serious glint in their depths making her wonder what woman would ever be so foolish as to withhold anything from him.

"I don't think I could if I tried." She lifted her hips, accepting him even deeper inside. "I've never been so out of control."

Whether he believed her or not, it was true. Their night together was so much more than she'd expected.

He withdrew from her then, part of the way, the agonizing loss of him only making her delight in his full return as he thrust into her again. Again. Each time raising the stakes for the release building inside her once more.

"Stay that way," he whispered, his words tickling

against her ear as he moved. "You look beautiful when you're out of control."

And just like that she lost it, his sweet words touching her as profoundly as any physical caress. But combined with that corporal contact, too, the O staggered her, wrenching a cry from deep in her throat. She convulsed with sweetly erotic spasms, arms tightening around Devon as she shamelessly clung to him. His release hit him as she held on, his body tensing, steeling over top of hers.

They remained locked around one another for long minutes afterward, their breathing slowing, evening out until they matched one another in perfectly synched rhythm. The lure of sleep finally overcame her, drawing her into peaceful slumber in his arms as the first rays of dawn penetrated their tented sheets.

Total bliss.

Yet even in her dreams, she was plagued by unrest at the thought of telling Devon why she was really in town this week. She was a card-carrying member of Crazies 'R' Us.

Yeah, he was going to love that.

DEVON LOVED sleeping in.

His whole life he'd had to get up at the crack of dawn—for school, for work—but since insomnia kept him awake half the night, he'd always figured he functioned on less alert brain cells than the rest of the world. So the days he got to sleep in made him feel brilliant. Articulate. Awake.

And waking up next to a beautiful woman who liked living on the edge as much as he did only enhanced the experience. The feeling of well-being lasted until he blinked through to full consciousness and wondered how to handle the morning-after situation. Granted, last night was fantastic, but Jenny had definitely hedged about extending their time together.

Damn good thing he was rested enough to tackle the inevitable sticky issues that arose from sleeping with someone he didn't know very well. He half wondered if she'd expected him to slip out the door while she was dozing, but Devon had never been that kind of guy. Even if their night together proved to be a one-shot thing, he'd at least be here to say good morning and tell her what an awesome time he'd had.

Levering up on his elbow he took an inventory of her suite, noting details that had slipped by him in the candlelight and in his intense focus on her. Her room was the same size as his, a single bedroom suite with the bedroom connected by double doors that—when opened—made the space airy and contemporary.

Sleek modern touches like Lucite and the shiny marble countertops that he had in his suite were more softened in here though, and Devon found himself wondering if she'd brought along the fuzzy angora throw pillows he'd flung on the floor last night in his haste to take her on the couch.

It seemed a strange thing to do—to bring pillows to a hotel—but then again he'd never met anyone who shipped her sheets to a hotel ahead of time the way Jenny had. She lived up to her "deluxegirl" screen name with her extravagant extras. The candles. The music. Fresh flowers in small glass bowls by the entryway and more on the coffee table.

A case of bottled water on the kitchen counter. A lot of little pill bottles, too. Vitamins, maybe?

Aphrodisiacs? It wouldn't surprise him with her. She seemed to enjoy sex more than any other women he'd ever been with. Although perhaps that wasn't a fair comparison since he'd only been with his wife in the last five years and his memories of encounters before then were hazy. And since Lori thought sex messed up her hair too much, he'd wearied mighty fast of only being allowed to touch her the night before her weekly spa day.

Here, signs of Jenny were everywhere, unlike in his hotel room where he tucked his shaving kit back in his suitcase when he wasn't using it. A tad obsessive, now that he considered the habit. A leftover impulse to control and order his world from back in the days when…

Shit.

He needed to quit living out of a suitcase and start making bigger messes. The idea of the past having any control over him now took a little sheen off his day of sleeping late.

"You look like a man in the throes of fierce morning-after regret." Jenny's sleep-husky voice drifted up from her pillow. "I swear I don't bite in the bright light of day."

Chasing away darker thoughts, he tore his eyes from the pill bottles near the sink. Could be ginseng for all he knew, although he hoped nothing was wrong with her. She seemed so vital and healthy.

"No biting?" He swiveled to peer over his shoulder. "I might have some teeth marks that disagree with you on that."

"Hardly." She reached for one of the bottles of water on the nightstand where he'd already noticed a second stash. Sitting up enough to take a sip, she pointed toward the wall near the sofa. "Although I think the guy in the room next door might have gone in for some biting. Did you hear all that moaning and yelling in the middle of the night?"

He shook his head. "Too busy shouting myself hoarse in this room. Although now that you mention it, I do remember the pictures on the wall vibrating, so they must have been trying to outdo us. Little did they know what a wild woman you are in bed. They couldn't possibly compete."

"I'm never a wild woman." She capped the water and dismissed his comment with an airy wave of her hand. "You just happened to catch me at a really unusual time in my life."

Shifting position, her movements grew stiff

somehow. Deliberate. She seemed to take her time placing the water bottle exactly where it had been on the nightstand.

The timing was pretty unusual for him, too, since he was walking away from his company and the last tangible connection with the man who'd mentored him. A decision that still left him uneasy. But something in Jenny's manner put him on alert.

"I hope *you're* not having any morning-after regrets."

"I'm not." She reached for her red flannel robe at the end of the bed and Devon realized he'd picked up all their discarded clothes the night before. "But I'm afraid you might once you find out how much of a wild woman I am *not*."

"I don't get it." It seemed sleeping in hadn't given his brain cells a boost today after all. "What do you mean?"

"I'm agoraphobic." She flashed him a halfhearted apologetic smile. "But I got off easy overall since my mom is probably borderline certifiable. Nothing she has is genetic though. I just have a case of the heebie-jeebies about leaving home."

"Agoraphobia." Devon frowned. "Fear of situations you can't escape from, right? Planes, subways, anything that makes you feel penned in?" He wondered if it just meant she couldn't do roller coasters, which might have accounted for her interest in them. "If this is about the coasters, it's no big deal—"

"Actually, I'm afraid to go most places." The words burst from her as if she couldn't hold them back another second. "The only reason I psyched myself up to come here is the self-help seminar being given by a renowned psychiatrist who's had good luck with agoraphobics. But it took weeks of planning and preparation and even then I had to drag half my house with me so I wouldn't freak out— What are you doing?"

Head spinning, Devon hadn't even realized he'd reached for his pants.

"Just—" dressing "—processing."

"It's okay." She handed him his shirt, her expression a combination of disappointment and maybe— relief? "I told myself last night that even if you were upset about the agoraphobia that at least I would have the time of my life."

He couldn't quite take in what she was saying, his brain still stuck on one question.

"Are you saying you're pretty much housebound most of the time?" He buttoned his shirt up slowly, staring hard at each button while he listened to her response and tried to reconcile what she was telling him about herself with what he'd observed firsthand last night.

The two didn't mesh. Did they? Memories of her shipping her sheets to the hotel ahead of time argued that maybe it made sense after all. Except that she was obviously nothing like his mother—thank God.

Sigmund Freud was probably laughing his ass off in the great beyond.

"Not totally." She paused and Devon forced his gaze up to look at her, arms folded around herself as she pushed up off the bed. "Actually, from your perspective, I probably am. I force myself out for a little walk once a week so I don't get complacent. I'll challenge myself to do new things like sit on the swings at a park or buy a bratwurst from a street vendor, but each time requires a lot of psyching myself up."

Devon didn't even know where to begin. She didn't leave the house more than once a week? Even with that, her outings sounded like she stuck to the most commonplace experiences.

But then, hadn't Jenny already said she understood if he wasn't okay with this? And there were no two ways around it, this wasn't okay for him at all.

At the mere mention of being housebound, the need to get outside rode him so hard he thought he might break out in hives if he didn't breathe in the cold March air blowing off the Atlantic right now.

"I'll, um—" His feet were already walking without his explicit permission, but damned if he could think right now. "I'll get in touch with you this afternoon. I'm late for a seminar."

A very uncouth move, he knew. But his head would explode if he didn't get outside *now*.

"I had fun." Jenny's voice seemed far away as he grabbed his jacket.

Damn.

"Me, too." His gentlemanly instincts forced his feet to retrace his steps and give her a kiss on the cheek. "I'll call you."

Devon didn't begin to know if he meant it, but one thing was certain. After spending most of his youth cooped up inside with his mother who would never leave the house, he could never get into a relationship with a woman who was reluctant to walk out her own front door.

5

JENNY MOORE—Killer of Libido.

She didn't really care for the new label, much preferring the manhunter title she'd given herself the night before. But alas, sometimes the cold, hard facts of morning-afters had to be faced and she couldn't deny Devon's complete and hasty retreat meant she'd stomped out any hope of future sexual encounters.

Pausing in the middle of ironing her clothes—a pantsuit with low riding trousers and a yellow camisole under the jacket—she set the iron aside and plunked down on the bed where they'd rolled around in flower petals the night before. Funny how not even the lure of a cute new outfit could cheer a woman when a man had dumped her.

She brushed away a handful of crushed roses, grabbing her conference booklet outlining the scheduled workshops for the day. The morning session was out of the question since she'd slept through it. But she could still snag some afternoon seminars and make the most of her conference experience.

Focusing on the typed grid of speaking panels and discussion groups, Jenny ignored the fact that every breath she took seemed tinged with lush floral scents. She would never be able to inhale the combination of gardenias and roses again without thinking of Devon Baines and their night together.

Could she be much more of a freaking sap?

Clutching the conference booklet more tightly—as if somehow that would help—she scanned the list of workshop titles starting in ten minutes. Manic No More: The Guided Imagery Cure. Hypnotize Your Way to Mental Health. The Tough Love Approach to Facing Phobias.

A smorgasbord for the dysfunctional.

Deciding the seminar about confronting fears might help and that she damn well needed to shake off her disappointment with Devon so she could take away some self-help strategies, Jenny turned off the iron and slid into her warm, pressed clothes. She plucked up a notebook and a conference ID badge on her way out the door, where she—hello—bumped into the man who'd been the first in line to give her the old heave-ho this week.

David Brady.

He looked as startled as she felt. But only for a moment. His expression quickly morphed into a warm smile that seemed deliberately charming.

"Jenny. What a nice surprise. Is this your room?" He looked surprisingly pleased to run into her for a man who'd purposely pawned her off on a colleague the night before.

The jerk. Could he have hoped to embarrass her or make her uncomfortable with his little joke?

Seizing the opportunity to make sure he knew *that* wasn't the case, she smiled coolly and headed for the elevator. No, damn it. Make that the stairs. She really needed to conquer the stairwell before she left the hotel. Then again, why challenge herself on a morning when she was already feeling adrift?

"Jenny?"

Planting her feet in the middle of the corridor, she refused to go farther until she'd solved the stairs/elevator dilemma.

And until she'd made sure David knew his juvenile trick had backfired.

"I'm glad I ran into you so I could thank you personally for giving me your friend's e-mail address. He's just my type." She tapped her chin in pretended thought. "You know come to think of it, I'd better run back to my room to grab the jacket that he left last night. See you around."

Had he actually spluttered as she walked away, or was that just wishful thinking on her part? Jenny couldn't be certain, but she knew the warm sense of satisfaction inside her would soothe her long enough to ensure she got to her workshop with a smile on her face—no matter whether she opted for the stairs or the elevator.

ANGER BUBBLED to the surface while David forced himself to leave the tenth floor corridor, his movements brittle with resentment as he jabbed the elevator button, accidentally clanking the ruby in his ring against the metal plate. Did the woman—a woman he'd thought of highly enough to pursue—mean to make him jealous even though *he* had dumped her?

He'd cultivated dozens of cyber relationships over the years in an attempt to share and hone his bedroom skills, but until he'd met Jenny, it had never occurred to him to search for a woman who might be worthy of him as a wife or a long-term lover. And although he hadn't recognized Jenny's potential in that department until late last night, he still knew she could be persuaded to see he was ten times the man Devon would ever be.

What the hell had he been thinking to give her another man's contact information? At the time, he'd thought he'd been doing her a favor by giving her boring Devon's e-mail. But now…

Had she honestly slept with David's rival last night while David had been getting a little too overenthusiastic with Sasha the S and M queen? The thought ripped through him so hard he wasn't sure he'd be able to attend his next conference session and smile politely at a bunch of pompous engineers who thought they were all smarter than him.

With one hand jammed in his pants pocket, he gripped his car keys so tightly that one of the sharp points threatened to penetrate the surface of his skin. Devon Baines had been a nonstop source of frustration for David ever since the first night his father had brought home his geeky engineering protégé to show off at the dinner table. Devon went to Rensselaer Polytechnic. Devon had earned every stupid grant and scholarship available to someone in the industry.

And most insulting, Devon's arrival ensured David would never gain his old man's approval—or financial backing—for any of the businesses David had wanted to start. If anything, Devon's supposed engineering genius had rekindled his father's love for his work and sealed David's fate as second rate.

But that was all in the past.

He'd proven his superiority by making sure the board chose him instead of Devon. And he could woo any woman—especially someone refined like Jenny— away from someone as crude and uncultured as Baines.

Stalking out of the conference hotel and into the parking garage on the other side of the street, David welcomed the chance to get the hell out of Quintessence for a few hours to get himself and his anger under control. If Jenny Moore had thought to make him jealous by using Devon as her shining example of manhood, she'd made a grave mistake.

Lucky for her, David would be only too glad to

teach her otherwise once he found a place to spirit her away for a more private rendezvous.

"How can you just walk away and leave us at the mercy of the imitation Brady?"

Staring out over the ocean from his seat on a bench outside of Quintessence, Devon had to smile at his colleague's use of their old nickname for Dave in the days before he'd convinced the board to give him a shot at running his father's company. Marwan Ben Saqr had been with Shore Engineers for as long as Devon, and the two had been friendly rivals since college. When they'd both ended up working for John Brady in the days Shore was just getting off the ground, they'd shared the same admiration for the guy.

"The board had the facts in front of them, Mo, same as we did. They knew I had more time in the field and more experience from a research perspective, too. They're more interested in bringing in business, and frankly, Dave Brady has…networked a lot." A gust of cold wind rolled over the boardwalk, stinging his eyes with an unexpected blast of sand kicked up from the beach.

"You mean he's kissed a lot of butts." Marwan—Mo—turned his back to the air stream as he bit off a curse. "I hate office politics bullshit and you know it. That's not why I got into this business, Devon. I don't know what the board is thinking to bring in a guy with no engineering skills to think of, but at this rate, we'll be lucky if we're not all out of work by next Christmas."

Devon had thought the same thing all along, but the sentiment had more bite to it when delivered by a colleague whose opinions he respected. Devon knew part of his own frustrations were personal, more so after what Brady had done to Jenny.

But Mo's opinions were more objective.

And *still* mirrored his own.

"I can start a new business." Devon hated the thought of such a talented group of people, hand-picked by the elder Brady for the skills and interpersonal dynamics they brought to the company, being scattered to the four winds. "I was going to start some private consulting, but if I can solicit a couple of big projects—"

"That's great, Dev, but it doesn't save the pensions, the company investment plans, the benefits we've accrued." Mo shrugged as he checked his watch, a medallion-sized timepiece with more features than most people's PDAs. "It's fine for you since you don't have kids and a family, but most of the people at Shore can't afford to gamble on a small company at this point in their careers."

Frowning, Devon wondered if he'd made a mistake in not fighting the board's decision to give Dave Brady the reins. He'd never considered his pride might hurt a lot of other people.

"You know any reason someone on the board would feel indebted to David?"

"Hell no. They all knew how much John struggled to bring him in line and how the kid paid his old man back by screwing up all the more in school and banging any maid or assistant John brought home. The board members ought to know better than most what he's like." Mo shook his head, obviously disgusted. "But I gotta get inside. I'm giving a talk on continuum approximation in five minutes."

"See you, Mo." Devon wished he could offer up something more concrete, but he didn't know where to take the old silent battle of wills with Dave Brady anymore.

Devon had given up talking to Dave outside work hours a long time ago since the tension between them was so thick you didn't need two X chromosomes to sense it. Another reason Devon figured they'd never be able to work in the same corporate structure for long. They flat-out couldn't communicate.

A problem Devon didn't seem to be having with Jenny Moore.

Wandering away from the hotel and casino, he edged around a couple of rolling chair guys hoping for a fare to push around the boardwalk even though a biting chill laced the air. Atlantic City's answer to rickshaws, the rolling chairs looked sort of like oversized strollers for adults—big carts that two could share while a runner pushed.

Unlike most people hanging around Atlantic City this weekend, Devon relished the nip of the cold, appreciating the way the frigid air penetrated his clothes and cleared his head to remind him he was outside, free of the dreaded four-wall syndrome that had plagued him too often as a kid.

He knew he'd been an idiot to run out on Jenny this morning, but the suffocating effect of four walls had resurfaced with surprising swiftness at her first mention of her tendency to stick close to home. Now, descending a short set of wooden stairs emptying out onto a deserted shore, Devon let the cold sand invade his shoes as he walked, his steps sinking into the deep bed of soft beach.

He'd have to apologize to her tonight—as soon as possible in fact—since he'd acted on knee-jerk reaction and with zero sense of empathy for her situation. The phobia thing sucked. She must hate it, too, since she'd battled it enough to attend the self-help seminar this week.

Some publisher of self-help texts sponsored the thing and although the featured star of the show was the latest psychotherapy guru who preached a doctrine of retraining your brain, there were a hundred other workshops with titles such as The Self-Confidence Toolbox and Do-It-Yourself Hypnotherapy. Devon had taken a detour around the workshops once he'd gotten his head together this afternoon, but Jenny had been nowhere in sight.

Hell, he'd be up for Jackass of the Year if he'd scared an agoraphobic into staying in her hotel room for the rest of the week after she'd had enough *cojones* to get out of her house and seek some help. Making Jenny totally different from his mother, who hadn't ever really wanted to master her wheelchair so she could get out of the house more often.

Knowing he wouldn't be able to think about the problems at Shore Engineers until he'd apologized to Jenny for acting like a ten-year-old, Devon pivoted on his heel to seek out his laptop.

The incident with Jenny had helped him see that he still sucked at coping with controversy—another holdover from his mixture of guilt and resentment over his mother's accident and her ensuing fears since he'd never wanted to complain for fear of saying something to hurt her. And no matter how much he'd told himself that he was doing Shore a favor by bowing out with class and dignity, he could see now that his need to leave was more a case of old instincts kicking in.

No more. Right after he fired off a massive apology e-mail to Jenny, Devon would shake things up at Shore Engineers. If he still wanted to leave the company at the end of the week, it would only be on the condition that everyone on the payroll knew exactly what type of guy had been put in charge.

He expected both things—the apology and the shaking up—were going to be a hell of a lot more uncomfortable than the sand in his shoes. But Devon knew you couldn't put a price tag on clearing out your head and—finally—thinking straight.

DESENSITIZATION.

Jenny tapped her pen on her forehead at the back of Baccarat Ballroom A where the workshop—It's Not Such a Big, Bad World: Agoraphobics Come Out of the Closet—was taking place. She knew about desensitization, had read all the literature on treatments for her issues and regularly scanned the Web for new studies that might help. But until today, she'd dismissed desensitization as too risky, too time-consuming and, well, too scary.

Putting herself out there to face the fears one component at a time, forcing herself into the situations that scared her most so she could grapple with the panic and survive the ordeal had always sounded terribly primitive. What kind of psychotherapy basically said, "Get over yourself"?

Yet, as the workshop speaker's voice settled into a monotone after an hour of lecturing, Jenny couldn't help but consider desensitization again. After all, hadn't she already tried the technique to a certain extent in coming to the conference this week? She'd forced herself into a new social situation, a new town and a strange hotel because she'd needed the help so badly and she wanted a chance at meeting the guy she'd been communicating with online.

Pausing her rapid-fire tapping of her pen against her forehead when the woman in front of her turned around to glare, Jenny was amazed to realize that her need for sex drove her here every bit as much as her need for a cure. And, after having her need for sex fulfilled in surprising and far more satisfying ways than she'd ever imagined, she wondered what other situations she might be willing to risk— what chances she might take—for a shot at a repeat performance.

"Spider!" someone screamed from the front of the workshop, a terrified feminine shriek that had at least five people in the room leaping onto their chairs in absolute terror.

"Arachniphobics," the man sitting next to Jenny muttered under his breath, his disdain evident in his voice. He cupped his hands around his mouth to shout up to the front of the room. "Step on the freaking thing so we can get on with it."

But his yell was lost in the sea of screams as other panicked workshop attendees—people afraid of crowds, people afraid of raised voices, people afraid of pandemonium, God only knows who else—started running for the door in a veritable stampede of fear.

"Twits," the cranky man muttered as he slammed his notebook closed. "Do you think they'd all shut up if I told them I was a rage-aholic?"

Pulling herself from her thoughts of sex, Devon and desensitization, Jenny was surprised to take an internal survey and discover she wasn't the least bit frightened of the escalating noise, the running or the strange man next to her.

Maybe sex and thoughts of sex could be her new form of therapy?

"You think your rage could compete with their fear?" Jenny spared a glance over her shoulder at the woman crying and hyperventilating in the front row, her feet hopping around in circles on her chair in a chaotic dance. "I think the lady up front would take you out with one stomp from her sensible shoes if you tried to distract her from anything but her spider."

It ticked her off that any guy sitting in on a self-help seminar wouldn't already know that fears didn't have to be rational to be totally paralyzing. Who was he to judge others?

Cursing spiders and women and arachniphobics in particular, the man moved toward the exit along with the rest of the workshop attendees who weren't actively engaged in panic attacks or crying jags. Jenny moved more slowly, still trying to process her thoughts about the desensitization technique.

Maybe she was at a stage in her life where she was ready for it to work. Gathering her bag with her conference material and her laptop, she retreated from the wreckage of the Baccarat Ballroom to a love seat tucked in a nook near a bank of pay phones.

By deciding to sit there instead of scurrying back up to her room, she'd be desensitizing, right? The love seat qualified as a strange place. And the more new situations and untried spaces she put herself in, the more adept she'd become at vanquishing her own demons, damn it.

Heart pounding with excitement and only a pinch of fear, she claimed the open seat with a warm sense of triumph.

Take that, phobia.

She fought the stray longing for something of her own to lay over the small sofa. Her favorite sheets. A throw. A handful of those rose petals she and Devon had rolled around on last night.

On second thought, maybe the bare love seat in the middle of a crowded hotel was just fine as is. No sense reminding herself how amazing sex had been when she'd scared off her one-night lover.

Wrenching open her laptop, she thought to lose herself in work via the hotel's wireless capabilities. Checking her e-mail, she scanned two dozen new messages, mostly vendors and clients for De-Luxe forwarded by her assistant. Seventy-year-old Mr. Serivolo actually preferred "senior administrator" for a title, but Jenny had a tough time observing protocol with a guy who'd been her next-door neighbor for twenty-some years.

He and his wife had moved in when Jenny was a toddler, their friendship becoming stronger when Joe Serivolo lost his wife to emphysema the same year Jenny's mom checked herself into permanent residence at an exclusive community living center.

Joe could have run the whole company with one

hand tied behind his back, but after forty-five years
as a car dealer and eventually a small business owner,
he preferred to defer to Jenny, saying he liked being
able to shirk off all blame for things that went wrong.
Jenny was about to address a few issues that had
come up with a delayed order from a Malaysian
vendor when another e-mail dropped into her inbox.

From db@shoreengineers.

Jenny debated ordering a drink before opening it,
her nerves suddenly in an uproar. But when she tried
to wave over a dark-haired cocktail waitress making
the rounds of the seating areas in this part of the
hotel, the woman scurried off in the other direction.

The same woman who'd waited on her and David
last night, too. Did he give her a bad tip? Jenny didn't
have a clue what drinks cost at a bar these days.

Unwilling to relinquish the corner of the love seat
she'd staked out to hunt down a glass of wine, Jenny
settled for taking a deep breath and clicking open
Devon's message.

I acted like an ass this morning. No two ways
about it. I don't blame you if you don't want to see
me, but I do have a lame reason for pulling the
Road Runner stunt this morning if you come down
with a case of morbid curiosity and care to hear it.

I admire you showing up at the hotel this week
despite the phobia. That took guts.

First round is on me—hell, all rounds are on

me—if you'd like to talk about the finer points of mechanical engineering behind the thrill rides at Atlantic City's Steel Pier. I'm going to check out the Ferris wheel tonight and see if I can talk someone into firing it up. Then again, if you'd rather stick close to the hotel, let me know.

I'd like a shot at apologizing in person—no strings.

Devon

Jenny tapped the delete key without actually hitting the button. She had to admit she appreciated a man who knew when an apology was called for. Everyone made mistakes, right?

Except mistakes like the one Devon made had the power to hurt her at a soul-deep level. She wasn't your average woman with a well-adjusted sense of self. She was a walking melting pot of neuroses.

Okay, maybe that overstated the case.

She might not be the basket case that her mother had become over the years, but Jenny knew traumatic personal relationships could wreak havoc with her goal to take her company public and conquer the agoraphobia once and for all. Did she want to make things harder for herself by connecting with Devon, who by his own admission, could be completely insensitive?

All her life, the need to protect herself—from her mother's strange mood swings, from people's perceptions of her mother and, eventually, from the fears that wanted to eat away at her very existence—had been a mainstay of her happiness. But as her finger slowed its thoughtful tap over the delete button, Jenny wondered if maybe she'd been giving that need too much sway over her day-to-day existence.

Being with Devon had opened her to new experiences, desensitizing her to his presence at a rapid rate because she wanted him so badly. She'd taken a huge risk to let him stay with her last night, and the consequences had been scary at first as she'd battled paralyzing fear. But then again, she had some sizzling memories to ward off the hurt of him leaving so abruptly.

Would it be foolish to think she should risk spending an evening with him for the chance to broaden her horizons a little more? And—oh God— maybe even venture outside the hotel?

The thought made her stomach clench but somehow the staccato beat of her pulse at the thought of seeing Devon again mitigated the fear.

Holy hysteria, desire was *way* better than a drug.

Devon Baines may have turned her from agoraphobic into sex addict in the course of one incredible night. Putting her fingers to the keyboard, she licked her lips and typed her response.

You're buying? Better bring your wallet, Baines. But I'll warn you, it's been a long time since I indulged my love of cotton candy and fried dough, so this date could seriously cost you.

I'll be at the Ferris wheel at 11 p.m.
Jenny

Her finger hovered over the Send key for a moment, but as she peered around at the next round of workshop attendees heading into the Baccarat Ballroom for a session labeled Finding Your Own Remedies Through Past Life Regression on the easel out front, Jenny knew she'd found her most promising remedy already.

Hitting Send with relish, Jenny counted on the lure of sex and Devon to motivate her right out of her comfort zone and into the real world.

6

"YOU'RE LATE."

Devon skidded to a stop in front of the Ferris wheel at 11:15, prepared for Jenny to have already left and grateful as hell that she hadn't.

"You know how slow these guys with the rolling chairs can be? I think I could have run here faster." He pulled a single gardenia blossom from his shirt pocket where he'd jammed it on his way out of the hotel earlier. "But at least I remembered to bring you this. I'm sorry about this morning and I'm sorry to make you wait."

He'd held an impromptu meeting with one of the members of the Shore Engineers board this afternoon, not expecting the guy to agree wholeheartedly that Dave Brady might not be the right man for the job of running the company. Their conversation had given Devon a few new ideas for shaking things up, but it had slowed him down when he'd been in a hurry to fix things with Jenny.

"Pretty solid interpersonal skills for an engineer." Smiling, she took the blossom and sniffed, the breeze whipping strands of her hair across her cheek. "Thank you. And while I appreciate you leaving the door open for me to ask what sent you running this morning, I hope you don't think it's horribly superficial of me to say I'd rather look forward to tonight than to worry about what's already done. Is that okay with you?"

She didn't want to dig in his head? Ask him a thousand questions? Berate him for not being there for her after their night together?

"I don't think that's superficial at all." If anything, he appreciated her willingness to move on. "I'm just grateful you gave me a chance to make it up to you."

"We'll see if you're still saying that after we visit the fried dough stand." Twirling the gardenia between her fingers, she glanced around the boardwalk.

"What do you think?" He gestured behind her toward the Steel Pier where rides, games and cotton candy stands gave Atlantic City tourists something to do besides gamble. "It's not as impressive in the off season, but it's been an Atlantic City staple for decades."

"Jersey's answer to Coney Island." She tucked the flower in the buttonhole of her black wool coat that looked like something a longshoreman would wear. A skinny pink scarf wound around the collar while a pair of jeans showed off her long legs. "I like it."

"Too bad they don't run the rides in March." He took a step toward the Ferris wheel before remembering what a big deal this might be for her. "How are you doing? Are you okay being here?"

Only then, as he reassessed her in light of the phobia she'd admitted, did he notice the difference in her tonight, the subtle changes in her body language, her expression. High color in her cheeks could have been from the chill blowing in off the ocean, but coupled with her rapid breathing and inability to stand still, Devon got the impression she was more than a little nervous.

"I'm fine. Scared, but excited." She hugged her arms around herself, shifting from foot to foot as a handful of other insane tourists walked by them with beers and hot dogs.

He admired her drive to beat her fears even while he was forced to admit she had done a more effective job conquering her demons than his mother had managed. No matter how many times his mom had said she'd like to be more self-sufficient, to leave the house once in a while, she'd never been able to work up the courage to follow through on her goals.

Devon had to give Jenny credit for her warrior spirit in staring down the fear.

"There must be some place to grab a bite farther down the boardwalk." He slung an arm over her shoulders, as much to keep her warm as personal indulgence, he told himself. "And I brought my wallet."

"Then by all means, bring on the boardwalk fare. Because I don't get out much, I have great appreciation for the kinds of junk food you can't get at home. I'm crazy for carnival cuisine." She didn't object to his touch, inclining her head ever so slightly toward his arm as he caught the clean scent of her hair.

An hour later they settled into the bottom car of the Ferris wheel sipping steaming hot chocolate, their chosen aperitif after gorging themselves on cheese fries and cotton candy.

"Are you sure you're not going to get me in trouble with security?" Jenny peered around the boardwalk before resting against the back of the seat, clutching her cup. "I don't want to take a big risk to go out in a new public place only to end up in jail for trespassing." She flashed him a crooked, teasing smile. "I might never recover from the setback."

"I don't think they put you in jail for trespassing, but either way I'll take full responsibility and say I held you here against your will." He loved this Ferris wheel and wouldn't miss the chance to share it with a woman who seemed as drawn to the rides as him. She might profess fears of going out into the world, but maybe his interest in the thrill factor associated with amusement rides had piqued her curiosity as well.

"How kinky of you." She sipped her cocoa, but the large cup didn't quite hide her grin. "Now I'm tempted to call over security just to see how you carry out that particular scenario."

An unexpected bout of lust drop-kicked him.

Devon had never experienced such a sensation on

a Ferris wheel, even when the ride was in motion. He set down his hot chocolate, thinking he might need to brace himself if Jenny kept tossing out comments like that one.

"How can a woman with a phobia be so fearless?" He hadn't expected to address that dichotomy just now, since all he really wanted to do was kiss her. But the words leaped out, giving voice to something he didn't understand about her.

"I'm not fearless, believe me." She ducked deeper in her seat, feet sliding forward on the gritty, sand-covered floor as the wind picked up again. "You don't know what I went through tonight to force myself out the door to be here."

"But you're here. Which means you had to trot out a hell of a lot more courage than me since I've never been afraid to go out my own door." He shouldn't have been so quick to shut her down this morning when she was explaining her issues, but he'd super-imposed his past on her and couldn't see beyond it to understand her. "But when I said you were fearless, I meant about sex. Not many women would use a bondage image as an opportunity to flirt after knowing a guy for less than twenty-four hours."

"Bondage?" She looked vaguely scandalized. Very vaguely, damn her.

Devon burned inside and Jenny sat there as cool as you please as if she'd forgotten about the ex-change. All around them, the lights of the boardwalk and the hotels and casinos lining it gave the night skyline a glittering, multicolored glow.

"Me holding you against your will," he reminded her, suddenly thirsty for her and to hell with hot chocolate. He pried her cup from her fingers to place it on the floor of the ride. In the distance, the rhythmic sound of waves rolling onto the beach merged with the chatter of visitors brave enough to face the early spring weather.

"Oh." She licked her lips as her gaze darted to his face. "I made an interesting discovery about me and sex today. Well, I think I figured it out last night, actually."

"Sexual discoveries can be good." He never would have expected the woman who'd hyperventilated in his arms just yesterday to have turned into a bedroom adventuress, but he'd give anything to get her alone again. "Did this realization have anything to do with me?"

His eyes held hers and he wondered if he communicated half as much need with just a look. She toyed with the ends of her pink scarf, winding the fabric around her wrists and bringing to mind exactly how he'd restrain her if they were to play out the game they'd been dancing around.

"As a matter of fact, it did." She shifted in her seat and the cart rocked subtly beneath them. "For some reason, sex seems to provide the extra incentive I need to make me brave. To take chances I normally wouldn't ever dare."

"Meaning you're ready for more adventurous sex,

or that sex makes you adventurous in other ways?" He was damn lucky he could breathe at the thought of taking sex to another level. He'd told himself that he had no expectations of this night other than getting a chance to apologize, but now that he was with Jenny again, he knew he'd been lying to himself if he thought that's all he wanted.

"Um. Wow." She smiled, a coy grin that seemed half seduction and half innocence. "I meant that the promise of sex seems to give me courage in other areas of my life. I never really gave any thought to more daring forms of intimacy."

She swallowed, her focus seeming to blur as she—he supposed—considered the possibilities.

"Sort of dazzles the senses, doesn't it?" Despite accusations to the contrary, he'd never been the kind of guy to really push the boundaries in the bedroom, content with straightforward sex. A little oral tossed in the mix to keep things interesting.

But now, with Jenny proposing provocative food for thought and actually considering the possibility of trying new things, Devon wanted nothing more than to be her partner for any and all experimenting. One of the boardwalk's rolling chairs would never get them back to their hotel as fast as he'd like.

"I don't know." She caught her lip with her teeth and he wondered what scenarios she might have envisioned to make her hesitate. "What did you have in mind?"

He bit back the urge to kiss the soft fullness of her

mouth, knowing once he had the taste of her on his lips he wouldn't be able to stop. The need to strip away all her clothes, to possess her again, more than he had the night before, rode him hard.

"I didn't have anything particular in mind." He wanted to hear what *she* wanted. What she fantasized about. "I'm just suggesting there are a lot of possibilities open to people who are willing to take chances."

"Have you ever—" she twirled the end of her scarf around her hand as she seemed to consider her words "—thought about a public place as an option for intimate relations?"

Holy. Hell.

Devon knew she couldn't mean here and now. It was freezing out, for one thing. Forty-five degrees, give or take.

Although if they settled deeper into the cart, the wind wasn't so much of a factor….

"Sure, I've considered it." Even now he began to predict the necessary logistics of a Ferris wheel encounter. Legs here, bodies there…or her on his lap…definitely doable. "Public sex elevates the taboo factor. Ups the risk of getting caught."

"Exactly." She shook her head, brow furrowed and Devon figured she'd already discounted the idea.

Damn.

"You don't want to take more risks."

She'd probably reached her quotient by coming out to the pier.

"No. It's not that. I just wonder why—with a lifetime of uptight fears breathing down my neck— I still really want to try something so risqué."

Devon couldn't move the half-finished cups of cocoa out of the cart fast enough. Pulling Jenny on his lap and into his arms, he figured this was one fantasy of hers he could make happen.

"I don't know, but I'll be damned if you'll go home disappointed."

JENNY DIDN'T fully process what Devon had in mind until her hip grazed the rock-hard length of him when he hauled her across his thighs.

Ooh.

Earth to Jenny. She shouldn't be surprised given the direction of their conversation, but she honestly hadn't been thinking about right here. In a Ferris wheel cart on a semideserted pier in Atlantic City, for crying out loud. No one seemed to get too close to the rides since they were closed, but still, there were people around.

Eating, playing arcade games, looking out at the water.

Devon bent to kiss her neck, sweeping her hair aside with his warm, broad palm. His lips heated her skin while the idea of what he wanted to do warmed the rest of her. She'd been nervous all evening, worried about panic attacks or bursting into spontaneous screams if she got too scared about being in a strange place. Yet strangely, the idea of getting naughty with Devon—here, now—soothed those nerves while stimulating others in a far more pleasurable way.

"I'm wearing jeans." She hadn't dressed for seduction, although now she wished she had. Her heart hammered louder than the waves slapping the nearby shoreline.

"I've studied the problem, accounted for the variables and I'm confident I can work around it." He tipped her head to the side to give himself all the more access to her neck. His tongue stroked hot circles down her throat to the V of her coat.

"You sound awfully sure of yourself." Her eyes slid closed as she gave herself over to him, trusting him instinctively.

"It's all simple mechanics and equilibrium." He unwound her scarf and freed the buttons on her coat. "I won't even let you get cold."

Jenny couldn't imagine how that could work, but then he dipped to kiss the cleavage exposed by an Indian-inspired gauze blouse. Her head fell against the cradle of his arms, her spine arching as she offered herself up to the warmth of his mouth.

Somehow the heat of Devon and what he wanted to do with her kept her warmer than the coat. She burned where he touched her, sizzled where he kissed. The cart shifted as he eased her lower until she was half-sprawled over his lap and the bench that he'd covered with her silk scarf.

Thoughtful.

Sexy.

And somehow the contrast of the hard seat made the silk of the scarf all the more luxurious, while the chill in the air heightened the sensation of heat in Devon's skin.

His hand speared down into her blouse and under the lace of her bra to cup her bare breast. He rolled the nipple between his fingers, tweaking it, making her hum with pleasure.

Somewhere along the pier a boom box waged war with the music from one of the arcades. Heavy metal versus techno. Two of her least favorites. But the grating sounds of angry guitar and synthesizers drowned out the bursts of laughter and muted voices of passersby.

No one could see them when they stayed low along the bench seat, and foot traffic was dwindling now that it was past midnight. If someone caught a glimpse of naked breast now and then, so be it. For a chance to conquer her fears and indulge in immediate gratification, Jenny was willing to risk a peep show. Being daring made her heart pound faster, fueled her hunger for him.

"These are so beautiful, Jen." His eyes glittered darkly as he stared down at her bare breasts, a silver ankh medallion dangling between them at nipple level. "So pink. So sweet."

He licked each one in turn, sending tremors of

pleasure through her and sweeping away her fears about being in a strange place. She didn't care where she was as long as she could have this heat, this constant state of arousal Devon seemed to be able to create for her so effortlessly.

"I want more." She huffed with excited pants, her breath condensing into white clouds in the night air.

"Be specific." He teased the erect points of her nipples with the necklace, trailing the medallion over each and dragging the little links of the chain across her supersensitive flesh. "Engineers don't think in vague terms."

"More nakedness." Her clothes restrained her when she wanted to wrap herself around Devon. Pushing herself upright, she wanted Devon more than she wanted to ensure total privacy. "And more touching."

"I can get you more naked." He was careful to keep the coat around her shoulders even as he swept aside her blouse and released the snap on her jeans. "But where do you want me to touch you? Here?" He skimmed a heart-stopping caress over the front of her lace panties. "Or here?" Unzipping her jeans, he reached deeper, but still only grazed the inside of her thigh.

She twitched restlessly on his lap, wriggling against the restraining denim even though he'd peeled them down a little. Guiding his hand between her legs, she cupped his fingers against the damp lace.

"Here. I need you to touch me right here." She

wrapped her arms around his neck, heedless of where her coat might fall in the hunger to feel more of him. "Beneath the lace."

She nearly came right out of her skin when he shoved aside the fragile fabric to touch her just the way she wanted. The wind between her coat and bare back only made her feel deliciously exposed, naked and ready for whatever the night had to offer. Her breasts pressed against Devon's chest anyway, so even if someone was watching…

But no one was watching. Their darkened hideaway was well out of the line of sparse foot traffic. And her need was too great to ignore.

"You like that, Jen?" His whispered words enflamed her, sent her hands on a quest down to his fly so she could repay the favor.

"I like it so much I want to give you the same pleasure." She fumbled with the buttons, the fabric impossibly stretched with the bulge beneath. "But first I want to come this way. I'm so close, Dev, and I—"

Her fingers ceased their journey as his hand picked up speed in its skillful manipulation of her clitoris.

"I'm going to make you come so hard you'll see stars with your eyes closed, but you have to promise not to scream."

She was beyond promising anything, her thighs tense and her whole body poised for the inevitable. When he bent to draw on her nipple while he touched her, her back bowed, the pleasure spilling through

her, blindsiding her. He kissed her, catching her cries
to ensure her silence since she couldn't have held
them back. The bite of the night air, the heat of their
bodies and the dizzying glow of lights from the
Atlantic City strip gave the whole experience a
surreal feel. Except it had been very real, her heart
still galloping.

"I want to give you something special in return,"
she whispered, dazed with the taste of his kisses and
the adrenaline rush still flooding her senses. "Something no one but us will see, even if we are in the
middle of a public place."

DAVID ADJUSTED his binoculars along with his hand
on his crotch as he watched the tasty little spectacle
a hundred yards in front of him.

He'd paid the rolling chair driver a hefty sum for
a bit of privacy at the end of the Steel Pier, figuring
the guy wouldn't mind a break to grab a slice of
pizza while David indulged a rare opportunity for
erotic espionage, even if he resented *his* Jenny in
another man's arms.

Especially this man's.

He'd followed Devon Baines late this afternoon in
an attempt to see if Jenny had merely been trying to
make David jealous by tossing off a comment about
sleeping with his colleague. To his surprise and fury,
David's spying had paid off by alerting him to the
fact that Baines was secretly meeting with members

of the Shore Engineers board of directors. Apparently his father's protégé wasn't going to disappear quietly, but at least David had discovered the treachery early.

Now, he'd have to step up his measures to secure his place at Shore Engineers. David would need to meet his inside contact as soon as possible to make sure his position remained secure.

But little did David know that Devon's night would reveal even more treachery. After walking out of his unauthorized meeting with members of the Shore board, Baines had left the hotel for a trip to the Steel Pier where Jenny—an expert in fellatio if the look on Baines's face right now was any indication—had been waiting.

Any hopes of her innocence had fled when she'd started peeling off her clothes in a public place. Spoiling herself with a man who wasn't worthy of her gentle ways and delicate tastes.

Anger at Jenny, at Baines and most of all, himself, simmered beneath the surface as he watched the illicit encounter they'd arranged behind his back.

Leaning forward in his seat to see around the bar supporting the half roof of the rolling chair, David massaged his dick with a vengeance while he imagined what Jenny's lips were doing right now. Was she taking Baines deep in her throat? Or was she giving him a more ladylike blowjob with flicks of a skillful pink tongue?

The woman obviously had more of a taste for adventure than he'd expected to be going at it in a Ferris wheel cart. But truly, how long would a pretty package like Jenny be satisfied with whatever marginal pleasures Baines might have to offer? A luscious morsel like her deserved more variety to quench the voracious appetite for sex driving her to bare her tits in public for any passerby to enjoy.

As if called by his dirty thoughts she resurfaced from the floor of the cart, licking her lips in triumph. Oh, but David would never allow her to satisfy him that way. A real man would be too busy pleasing *her*. Didn't she understand that?

The thought of what *he* would do to Jenny Moore spurred his hand to work harder, faster. Baines seated her on his lap while both of them faced David's binoculars, bodies writhing together in a frenzy of need. No doubt Baines had slid inside her by now, boning her from behind with fierce thrusts that jiggled her breasts in licentious display for David's eyes.

Soon, it would be David's turn to be inside her and he would erase any memory of Baines's vulgar person from her mind and her luscious body. Then Jenny would be his again, sweet and innocent and hungry for him, the way she'd been when he first met her online.

At the thought, David came so hard he lost his focus, his expensive binoculars falling to the board-walk with a loud thud. Damned inconvenient that she had caused him to lose control here when he still had so many preparations to make for their inevitable private time together.

All alone.

But the incident only cemented what he already knew. First, he would make sure Devon Baines had no chance to steal his company out from under him after all his hard work to secure his place at Shore Engineers. Then, David would ensure Jenny Moore arrived in his bed as soon as possible so he could reform her ways with the kind of sexual finesse only he could offer.

7

"YOU KNOW what you need?" Hal McCormick, Shore Engineers second most senior board member, blew a smoke ring high in the air in his suite and then stared down his patrician nose at Devon. "You need some dirt on David Brady if you want to oust him. Too many members of the board want to vote with their hearts and they put John Brady's son in charge as a tribute, even if Dave is a little short on field hours."

"You should know I'm not trying to run a smear campaign here." The way he was beginning to wonder if David damn well had, Devon thought, frustrated all his efforts would come to this kind of stalemate. "I just want to make sure you're taking into account all the facts since it's not going to be much of a tribute to John if the company he busted his butt to build goes belly-up or gains a reputation for sloppy work. Hell, I'm going to go out on a limb and suggest that would piss him off."

Devon had lined up informal meetings today with all the board members except for two in an effort to get a better read on the facts. His conversation with

Mo and his own gut instincts told him it was better late than never to stick his neck out. Make an effort to be a team player. But the seniormost board member wouldn't be making an appearance at this week's conference and, from all accounts of his colleagues, Roy Scott had been Dave's biggest supporter in the decision to bring him aboard.

Devon would have far rather spent all week coaxing Jenny out of the hotel into new and tempting situations than to hang out here in a smoke-filled suite with a crotchety old engineer. Now that he knew the power of sex for her and her willingness to see what risks passion would lure her to take, Devon had to admit corporate politics seemed pretty freaking boring by comparison.

Still, he owed it to Mo and himself and everyone else at Shore Engineers to avert the potential disaster he feared Dave Brady represented. Brady's game playing with Jenny only reinforced Devon's long-standing gut feeling about the guy—that somehow Brady was a little off.

"I wish you'd made these points more forcefully to the board before the initial vote." Hal took a last drag of cigarette that was down to just a butt, inhaling deep before he stubbed the thing out in a cereal bowl at the kitchen counter littered with reports on vibration problems in a recent company project. "I pitched your case the best I could, Dev, but I think my recommendation would have been a whole lot more effective if you'd bothered to back yourself up."

"Jesus, Hal, I thought the numbers would speak for themselves. I've done ten times the work Brady has." Devon flipped idly through some of his colleague's papers, a sampling of Shore's biggest current projects. "What kind of business are we running if we don't listen to what's in black and white right in front of our noses?"

"Spoken like an engineer." Hal scooped up a handful of papers and jammed them into a folder before stuffing the whole thing into a briefcase. "Just remember, not all of the guys on the board think having a twelve-page résumé is enough for the head of the company. Being top dog requires salesmanship. Showmanship. An ability to recruit new business. For all his flaws, Brady has a certain amount of charisma. Hell, I don't particularly like the guy, but even I can see it."

"We're not running a popularity contest." Devon knew he ought to let it go since Hal was making for the door, but he couldn't wrap his head around why smart people would vote in a guy who'd flunked thermodynamics twice to lead an engineering firm. It didn't make logical sense. "Brady's own father gave up on him. What the hell kind of character endorsement is that?"

"John Brady liked you, Dev, so maybe you were never treated to the less than sunny side of the old bastard, but I'll tell you this. John was a hell of a lot better engineer than he was a father, you get me?"

Yanking open the door to the corridor, he held it wide for Devon.

"But why do personal politics have to play a role in something that should be so freaking obvious?" He couldn't let it go yet. "I'm not trying to brag, Hal. But I know what I'm doing out in the field and I don't think you can say the same for Brady."

"Personal politics always play a role in business, Baines." He clapped Devon on the shoulder. "I'll back you because I happen to think you're the better man for the job, but you're not going to make any headway with the rest of the board—especially Roy Scott, whose favorable opinion you need the most—if you can't start seeing beyond the integral equations and Fortran applications to the people behind this company."

Nice move, Dev.

He'd managed to tick off the one man firmly on his side. Roy Scott needed to be Devon's next visit since his opinion carried the most weight. Unfortunately, Devon had always tended to keep a wide berth from Roy since the guy's wife had a habit of hitting on him at every company picnic and family function at the office.

Yeah, he sucked at the social stuff.

Nodding stiffly, neck tense from the creeping knowledge that maybe he'd been missing a lot of the big picture, Devon headed for the door. He paused before he walked away, knowing he couldn't leave without reminding Hal of one last relevant fact.

"Your point is well taken and I appreciate the heads-up, but I can guarantee Shore is going to get no respect in the industry—showmanship or not—with a guy in charge who couldn't solve his own vector calculus problems if he had three hours and a goddamn calculator."

Stalking out, Devon had had all the meetings he could take for one day. Did the whole board of directors think he had his head up his ass when it came to people? Sure his skills as a butt kisser were lacking, but that's only because he'd never applied himself to the task, figuring his time was better spent designing the best possible mechanical applications for his clients.

He ignored a handful of people exiting the elevators and then wondered if that meant he was antisocial. Frowning at the thought, he wrenched open the door to the stairs and climbed to the tenth floor.

Jenny's room.

The answer seemed obvious, the only one that made sense in this particular equation. Jenny didn't care if he was antisocial. Hell, maybe that's why they'd hit it off. She was scared to go out, and he didn't really want to talk to anyone anyway.

What a screwed up pair they were. Okay, maybe him more than her. At least she had a medical justification for her reclusive ways. He, on the other hand, seemed to be a widely acknowledged son of a bitch if Hal's take on the situation proved correct.

Devon found himself in front of 1016, not even fully cognizant of how he'd gotten there. Rapping on her door, he waited for her light step or her soft voice or the lilting notes of whatever classical piece she might be listening to today. But his knocks were met by silence. No music. No Jenny.

Pivoting away from her empty suite, Devon was surprised by the stab of disappointment. He'd known her for two days and already he wanted to be with her more than anyone else in his life.

Could be a side effect of the phenomenal sex. Or could it mean something more?

He hastened his step, unwilling to consider the possibility when he needed to pour all of his energies into saving Shore Engineers and giving the board a better man to lead their company. And since he wouldn't be able to do that by hiding out in his suite all week, Devon headed to the elevator to search for any of his colleagues who might be roaming the hotel. He'd just have to wait until later to indulge his fascination with Jenny.

Lucky for him, he was an insomniac. He'd have plenty of hours to sort out the mystery of her allure for him and see what sexual scheme she'd cooked up next.

FIVE MORE MINUTES and then she could leave.

Jenny checked her watch for the second time in as many seconds, hating every moment of this stupid desensitization exercise that had her sitting in the middle of the hotel's lobby close to the bar all by herself. She'd chosen this insane method of exposing herself to new surroundings—brute force, basically—but as she watched the throngs of hotel guests and casino visitors come and go, she had to admit she'd despised the idea from the beginning.

It was one thing to challenge herself to conquer new places with Devon by her side and the utterly absorbing distraction of sex to engage all her senses, but to try this exercise on her own where no one knew her or knew to look out for her? What if she hyperventilated herself into a coma and the strangers around had no clue what to do with her?

Or what if she fainted from a bout of manic fear and she took a nosedive into the carpet where a thousand people's feet trod every day, exposing her face to countless germs and potentially giving the world a glimpse at her peacock-blue undies if her minidress with the flirty flounced hem didn't fully cover her butt?

Four more minutes.

To top it all off and make her feel even more neurotic than usual, she also had the distinct impression of being watched. Great. Now she could add paranoid delusional disorder to her list of defects. Sheesh, she needed to tap into some of her confidence when it came to dealing with customers.

Or dealing with Devon on a Ferris wheel.

But no amount of self-deprecation could ease the

sensation making her neck itch and her skin crawl. Her heart pitched faster in her chest, the piano music from the bar fading into background noise now as her ears could only focus on the raspy sound of her breathing. Cool currents of air blew in through the double doors every now and then as bellhops and valets jogged in and out of the main entrance with keys and luggage. Shivering from the want of Devon's warm hands on her body, she would *not* look at her watch no matter what.

God, she was pathetic.

"Can I take your order?" A waitress raised her voice, bending down into Jenny's line of vision to be heard.

The same waitress who'd flirted with David her first night here and then avoided her yesterday outside the seminar.

"Yes." Grateful for the interruption that forced her to think about something besides her sorry mental state, Jenny took out her wallet and focused on the other woman's wary blue gaze. "I'll have a sparkling water with lemon and I hope you'll accept my apologies if the guy I was with the other night left you a bad tip. I didn't really know him very well."

Something shifted in the woman's expression, her eyes growing still more shuttered and she'd visibly flinched at the mention of David. Strange. Unless someone had stepped on the back of her shoe at the same time. Entirely possible in this kind of crowd.

And wasn't the risk of having your shoe stepped

on a sound reason for preferring to stay in your hotel room all day?

"The tip was more than generous." Something about the woman's assurance didn't ring true, but Jenny couldn't figure out quite what. She was better with people through e-mail or via phone, seeing nuances in voices and writing in a way she was too nervous to comprehend during a face-to-face confrontation.

"Oh. Good." She smiled, nervous and hoping by the time her water came she could leave the lobby and lose herself in an all-night sexfest with a man who both scared and fascinated her at the same time. "I just didn't want you to think I was a lousy tipper by association and he turned out to be kind of a jerk."

"I'll say."

"Pardon?" Jenny's heart still swooshed so loudly in her ears she figured she'd misheard the woman— Sasha, according to her name tag.

"Nothing." The woman tucked her serving tray under her arm. "That was just a rough night for me, too. Guess it's true what they say about don't judge a book by the cover, huh?"

With no other explanation of her cryptic comment she sauntered off to another table, navigating the hectic landscape with grace despite her high heels. Jenny would give her eyeteeth to appear so at ease here, but she figured she was probably pale and sweating. Not a good look for her.

Two minutes and she was out of here, water or

not. Although she'd certainly pay the bill and leave a good tip anyway, just in case Sasha had been fibbing about David leaving her enough cash the other night.

Two more minutes and Jenny would hunt down Devon and haul him into the nearest vacant room and wrestle him out of his clothes. She'd lose herself in male muscles—Devon's muscles—and hard driving, don't-forget-who-you're-humping sex. Her temperature spiked just thinking about it and what she'd do next time she got her hands on Devon. The cool air gusting in from the doors didn't make a dent in the sudden steamy fog around her body, her thighs clenching instinctively to quench the ache.

"Jenny." His voice echoed right out of her thoughts and into her ear as Devon strode into view.

Clad in a sleek charcoal business suit with a lavender tie, he approached her seat at a small table with long, loose strides. Memories of the night before came flooding back, the crisp bite of the wind on her bare skin and Devon's arms banded around her to ward off the chill while she rode him.

Now, she couldn't quite find her voice to greet him since all she wanted to do was start peeling off his clothes. Feast upon him the way she had the night before.

"Damn it." Devon hauled her to her feet, his voice growling low and warm in her ear as the heat of his body penetrated her dress right through to her skin.

"Don't look at me like that unless you want to get a whole lot bolder with public displays of affection."

"Promises, promises," she whispered back, dumping a wad of bills on the table for the waitress and ready to play now that her five-minute desensitization exercise was over.

"Hell." Tucking her under his arm, he pulled her through the lobby around a spewing marble fountain and the concierge desk with guests lined up in front. His chin grazed her temple as he spoke into her ear. "I've been thinking about you all day."

"I think I'd be offended if you didn't after what happened last night." She didn't mind the crowd, didn't care about the strange terrain they covered as he guided her out of the lobby and down a side corridor toward the pool and the gym facilities. Devon filled her senses completely, leaving no room for outside impressions to kick-start her phobia.

"You've got an astonishingly talented mouth, I'll give you that." He passed the beauty spa and the pool area, the smell of chlorine and nail polish remover filling the hallway.

Jenny turned her head toward Devon, her lips grazing his neck as she inhaled the spicy scent of his aftershave instead.

"I'll bet you'd rather give me a whole lot more." She slipped her hand under his jacket to rest low on his hip. "Wouldn't you?"

She was so absorbed by the hard, muscular feel

of him under her hand and his hot, ragged breath in her ear that she didn't really notice where he was leading her until he veered sharply to the left, shoving open a door to a darkened room.

A large, empty dark room, judging by the way their footsteps echoed against the hardwood floor and bounced around the walls. Devon locked the door behind them with a soft click.

"Where are we?" Not that it mattered. And God, when had she ever been able to say that about her surroundings? That total lack of concern for her whereabouts was an agoraphobic's dream come true.

"I don't know. Squash court. Racquetball court, maybe. Something like that." He pressed her up against a padded wall to one side of the door, his lean, masculine body dominating hers with obvious strength. "There's a window looking in, but if we keep the lights off and stay to the side, we should be safe long enough to take the edge off."

"Mmm." Her fingers skipped up his chest, raking over him from abs to pecs. "Just what I need."

Her eyes had barely adjusted to the light, enough to see a vague outline of Devon but no more. His hands gripped her face, angling her jaw where he wanted, his thumb skimming her lower lip. She nipped him, sinking her teeth lightly into his skin before she soothed the spot with a suggestive swirl of her tongue.

"I dreamed about you last night. Dreamed about

this." He slid the wet digit down her chin and neck, pressing softly into the hollow of her throat.

"I didn't think I gave you any time to sleep last night." They'd walked back to the hotel well after 2:00 a.m. and then when he'd escorted her to her suite, their heated good-night kiss led to a quickie against the refrigerator. And then a not-so-quickie in her bed. "Remind me not to let you go back to your room before noon this time."

Her hands worked the buckle of his belt, shaking with impatience, desire and who knows what other emotions were tangling up inside her for Devon.

"I couldn't think straight all day." He walked his fingers down her hip, hooking the fabric of her dress higher and higher until he cupped her bottom with nothing but a bright blue satin thong to cover her gorgeous self. He groaned at the discovery of her mostly bare skin. "And now you've ensured I won't be able to think at all tomorrow either."

"No?" She shivered when he trailed a fingertip over the curve of her rump, her hands pausing on the fabric of his fly.

"I'll be too busy thinking about what a wicked woman you are, running around the hotel with nothing but this—" he tugged at the satin T-strap centered above her cheeks "—sorry excuse for underwear covering your sweet little ass."

The friction of satin stretched taut against her made her squirm. She couldn't think about anything besides having him touch her. Getting him inside her. She rubbed the inside of her thigh against the outside of his, bending her knee as she twined herself about him to give him better access.

"Please, Dev——" Her soft request was magnified by the empty room, her need amplified. The urgency in her own voice might have startled her at any other time, but she couldn't think about that now when his thumb marked a feathery X over her clit through her panties, so close and yet not nearly enough. "Touch me there."

"X marks the spot?" He sounded too damn sure of himself and she didn't care.

"Treasure's all yours if you'll just——"

He touched her then, his thumb sweeping aside the tiny satin triangle to expose her. He rubbed, circled, teased her with her own juices until her nails sank into his shoulders through the lightweight wool of his jacket. The sound of Dev's breathing filled her ears, his spicy male scent mingling with her gardenia fragrance and the scent of sex. Heat flamed inside her until she hovered seconds from release.

And then a phone rang.

Not his, not hers, but a cell phone right outside the door. Or maybe right outside the wall of Plexiglas looking into the darkened court from the corridor.

Devon froze and her heart stopped. They stood together, unmoving, while a masculine voice cursed a muffled obscenity and the ringing stopped.

"Can anybody see through that window?" Jenny

whispered, her eyes adjusted enough to the dark that she could make out the wall of clear plastic just to the right of the solid door. They were hidden behind the entryway, but if somebody in the hallway was at the right angle...

"They'd have to really be looking hard to see anything," he whispered back, releasing her and buttoning his jacket. "And they'd have to have their nose pressed right up to the glass."

She didn't say anything, but they both knew that the ringing cell phone had sounded as if it came from directly on the other side of the wall.

"Wait here." He opened the door out onto the hall, his broad shoulders and lean hips silhouetted by light flooding into the court from beyond.

She trembled in her high heels, partly from thwarted passion and partly from her personal issues roaring back to life with Devon moving away from her. Damn it. She needed more desensitizing.

Or an orgasm.

Preferably both.

"Come on." He motioned for her as he held the door open with one hand and dug his cell phone out of his jacket pocket.

He needed to call someone now?

Disgruntled and itchy to get back to where they'd been a few moments ago, Jenny followed him into the hall. The *empty* hall, thank goodness. She'd been a little nervous at the thought of someone spying on them.

"I can give you some privacy if you need to make a call." She wrapped her arms around herself in an effort to still her leftover tremors from so much coiled energy with no outlet.

Devon pushed buttons on the phone in silence, as if totally oblivious to her presence. She might have walked off in a huff, except that two seconds after Devon pushed Send on his phone, an answering ring sounded just around the corner.

8

DEVON SMASHED the End button on his cell phone, hoping he'd disconnected before caller ID kicked in. What the hell was Brady doing shadowing him around the hotel and lurking in dark corners? Had he heard rumors about Devon wanting to oust him from Shore Engineers?

Gripping Jenny's waist, he steered her in the opposite direction from where the telltale ring had come, toward the main elevators.

"Do you know who was outside the racquetball court?" She kept her voice at a discreet volume, peering over her shoulder toward the maze of locker rooms, saunas and steam lounges near the hotel gym.

"Yes." His hand flexed possessively along her hip. He figured she had a right to know if he'd inadvertently launched her into his power struggle with a colleague.

Then again, she had a connection to Brady that had nothing to do with Devon or Shore Engineers. Could Jenny's ex-cyber boyfriend be following her and not Devon?

They reached the door to the stairwell and he

wrenched it open, anxious to find someplace private to talk.

"Not the stairs." She halted in front of the door, unmoving. "I can't do stairs when I'm wound up."

Only then did he look at her, *really* look at her, and see the way her rapid breaths had her chest heaving and her hands fluttering restlessly through the air. She wasn't hyperventilating the way she had that first night when he'd walked into her suite, but she seemed close.

"No stairs. Got it." He let the door swing shut as he moved back to her side, trying to remember what had helped her settle down that first night. Holding her half-naked on his lap. Since that wasn't really an option for right now, he settled for squeezing her more firmly against him as they dodged casino visitors spilling into the hotel halls. "Just tell me what to do to help you relax. Can you take the elevators?"

She nodded and he edged around a small group of older ladies taking pictures of the hotel's nightly laser display on a fountain timed to music. Anger bubbled inside him like one of the gushing spouts, his frustration at Brady for spooking her threatening to spew at any moment.

"Is my suite okay, or do you want to go to your own?" He didn't know if she'd rather get somewhere private quickly or if her phobia demanded her own room, but he planned to make good on whatever she asked for.

"Either." Her word gasped out between shallow breaths.

An elevator ride later they were standing outside his suite while he swiped his keycard.

Green light.

Thank you, God. He ushered her inside, hoping—no, praying—she didn't pass out or anything. He wouldn't have the first clue what to do.

"I'm okay." She spoke quickly since the fast breathing phenomenon didn't give her much time to talk between huffs. "Really."

"Would it help to get naked?" He pulled her deeper in the room now that the door had closed behind them.

Her bark of laughter was unmistakable even if it was smothered in rapid panting.

"I'm serious." He loosened his tie and whipped off his jacket, tossing it on the kitchen counter as he tugged her toward an overstuffed armchair in the ultramodern living room with sparse, sleek furnishings. "I'm willing to make sacrifices for the sake of your health."

He scooped her up in his arms as he lowered himself into the chair, planting her on his lap. She started to speak but he hushed her with a kiss, just a brush of his lips over hers until she quieted. Stilled. Something about those silent moments with their foreheads touching and their breath mingling seemed deeply intimate, creating an illusion they understood each other, if only for a short time.

"Thank you," she whispered finally, her hand fisting in the fabric of his shirt. "I started to panic thinking you know someone who would follow us around."

He angled back to gauge her expression. Serious. Concerned. Still, he had no choice but to be honest with her.

"I do, and so do you." Devon wasn't willing to shoulder all the blame for Brady's interest in them as a couple. "The guy outside the racquetball court was Dave Brady."

"How did you know it was him?" Frowning, she released his shirt, her hand smoothing out the wrinkles. "I mean, how did you know to try his phone?"

"Lucky guess." He didn't see any need to bombard her with the details of his private meetings with board members this week and the way his company seemed to be dividing into two camps. Besides, mostly what tipped him off was gut instinct. Well, that and the disappearance of a distinctive ruby class ring around a corner farther down the hallway. "Plus the ringing sound that interrupted us in the court was the standard default tone on all the phones handed out by Shore Engineers."

"That sounds way too lucky to me." Her hand fell away from his chest. "You don't think he's still playing some kind of sick trick on me as a follow-up to giving me your e-mail address, do you? I mean, you'd think he would have better things to do with his time than pawn off a neurotic woman on one of his employees and then—" she narrowed her gaze "—follow them around to see what happens. Do you think he wanted to see how long it took before you lose your mind from hanging out with a crazy woman?"

Guilt nipped him for not coming clean about his maneuvers to overthrow Brady from the firm, but Devon didn't want to give her any more reasons to be stressed when she had to be coping with a lot just to stay in Atlantic City this week.

"You haven't seen him following you around before tonight, have you?" He stared down at her bare knees flung over the arm of the chair, the hem of her thin dress dipping between her legs. He'd rather be having any conversation with her besides this one. For that matter, what he really wanted was to skip over conversation altogether and slide his hand beneath her dress again, but they needed to get to the crux of the Brady problem first.

"No. Although he was in the hall outside my suite that first morning after you bolted."

"Did he say anything to you?" Devon told himself he didn't have any reason to be jealous, but that didn't make a dent in the surge of possessiveness that set his teeth on edge.

"I didn't really give him a chance." A wicked grin curved her lips. "I took the opportunity to thank him for passing along your contact information and told him you were just my type."

Some of the tension in his neck eased. "What did he say to that?"

"Hmm." She bit her lip. "Not much. I faked like I forgot your jacket in my suite—you know, to let on we'd spent the night together—and excused myself to retrieve it."

"So he knows we're seeing each other. Did he look annoyed?"

Devon's old mentor hadn't done him any favors by pitting him against his son from their very first meeting. Although, in all fairness, Devon had probably been quick to prove his loyalty to John Brady— and set himself apart from Dave—right from the beginning.

"By then I was starting to sweat about whether to take the elevator or stairs since I'm not keen on either, so I didn't really get a visual on him." She shifted slightly, her hip nudging him as she resituated herself. "I do remember thinking he made some sort of disgusted sound, but since he'd been so quick to toss me aside that first night, I didn't think he'd give a flying fig one way or another what I did with you. I just wanted to let him know I wasn't mourning his loss."

Devon couldn't imagine what Brady hoped to accomplish by following Jenny all over Quintessence Hotel and Casino. But then, Devon never had much luck thinking his way through problems that weren't related to numerical integration or differential equations. His brain worked like an engineer. Rational.

Linear. Straightforward. Trying to figure out this guy's motives for anything was sort of like reading blueprints backward and underwater. The lines didn't connect, didn't make sense.

"Why?" Jenny frowned down at him, tapping a finger against her chin. "I don't understand why he would give a rip about seeing us together."

"Let me ask you this." A vague idea took shape in his head. "Did he seem completely normal to you when you e-mailed him before this trip?"

"You think I'd bother hooking up with someone who seemed less than normal?" She wound her arms around his neck. And then froze. "Or are you asking if I thought he was a head case…like me?"

She angled back to check his expression, her arms falling away from him again.

Damn it.

"That's not what I meant." Although he wasn't sure he could explain what he did mean without pulling her deeper into his old feud. "And just because you sought a little self-help this week doesn't make you a head case. You wouldn't be running a successful start-up business single-handedly unless you were smart as hell and disciplined enough to make your vision a reality."

"You've got that right." She sniffed, tucking a few wavy strands of her hair behind one ear as she slid her legs off the arm of the chair and rose to her feet. "But if you didn't mean to suggest that Dave Brady related to me because we were both mildly crazy, what exactly *did* you mean?"

"I don't know." He watched her prowl restlessly around the room and wondered vaguely if she was uncomfortable in the new surroundings. But she'd said either suite was okay. And, selfishly, he couldn't help but appreciate the strides she seemed to be determined to make with her phobia by facing new surroundings. "I've always thought the guy was a little off, but then again I know I've never liked him, so I don't necessarily trust my judgment because I assume it's massively biased. I'm just curious what your take on him was when you met him online."

Well, *mildly* curious. True, he wanted to know, but as soon as the question fell out of his mouth he found himself battling down frustration at the idea of Jenny with Dave. A guy everyone but Devon and Mo seemed to find at least marginally charming.

Now, Jenny stood at the sliding glass door of his balcony, staring out into the U-shaped courtyard that housed an outdoor pool below. Even though it was too cold to swim, Devon had found himself staring out into that same courtyard before since the wraparound structure of the hotel afforded a view of a hundred other hotel room windows, and a bird's eye perspective into at least twenty other people's lives who couldn't be bothered to close their drapes.

"I'm usually a good judge of character through phone calls and e-mails since I rarely meet any of my

vendors in person for my business." Tipping her head
to the window, she lifted a hand to the glass as if she
could reach out and touch the view. "But now that I
think about it, I never spoke to Dave over the phone.
We traded e-mails for a few weeks and I convinced
myself I liked him because, yeah, he did seem
normal. Or at least normal for an online dating scenario—he didn't hide behind a fake name, he had a
real job with ties to the community."

He stalked closer to her and didn't bother turning
on the lights in his suite, preferring the dim illumi-
nation filtering through his open curtains to make
confidences easier. Plus, the dark allowed Jenny to
look out the window without anyone seeing her.

An anonymous voyeur.

The need to have her again, to finish what they'd
started downstairs, made his mouth go dry. But this
discussion seemed too important to postpone.

"Do you mind if I ask what attracted you to him
specifically?" He didn't know what perverse demon
made him pose the question. But he wanted to know
more about her, to understand this intensely private
woman who could run a major company with nation-
wide distribution from the anonymity of her apartment on the Jersey Shore.

And if that meant sucking it up while she thought
about what attracted her to someone else, then he'd
just have to find a way to take it like a man.

"He showed an interest in my business. And when

you're an entrepreneur, your business is your whole life, so right away that appealed to me." She turned her head against the glass door for a moment to cast him a sideways glance. "In fact, he mentioned wanting to start a side business of his own one day, so he had a lot of questions about the nuts and bolts of running a company solo."

"Did he? No mention of what kind of company he wanted to start in particular?" Devon processed that new bit of information, remembering that ever since Brady had been in college, he'd been trying to con his father into backing one home-based business after another in a series of get-rich-quick schemes. At least, that had been John's take on it. Now Devon wondered how biased his opinion might have been.

He stood a scant few inches behind her, well into her personal space, but refrained from touching. For now. After how fast things had heated up between them in the lobby and then on the racquetball court, he knew he couldn't touch her without peeling off her clothes.

"No. I meant to ask him more about the venture this week before I realized what a superficial twit he must be." She returned her attention to the myriad lighted windows in the wall of hotel rooms across the courtyard. "I see now that I made a mistake in not calling him before I agreed to meet him in person since you learn a lot about someone over the phone. I would have picked up on his...unusual personality quirks if I'd have spoken to him."

An Important Message from the Editors

Dear Reader,

If you'd enjoy reading romance novels with larger print that's easier on your eyes, let us send you TWO FREE HARLEQUIN PRESENTS® NOVELS in our LARGER PRINT EDITION. These books are complete and unabridged, but the type is set about 20% bigger to make it easier to read. Look inside for an actual-size sample.

By the way, you'll also get a surprise gift with your two free books!

Pam Powers

Peel off Seal and Place Inside...

THE RIGHT WOMAN

she'd thought she was fine. It took Daniel's words and Brooke's question to make her realize she was far from a full recovery.

She'd made a start with her sister's help and she intended to go forward now. Sarah felt as if she'd been living in a darkened room and some-one had suddenly opened a door, letting in the fresh air and sunshine. She could feel its warmth slowly seeping into the coldest part of her. The feeling was liberating. She realized it was only a small step and she had a long way to go, but she was ready to face life again with Serena and her family behind her.

All too soon, they were saying goodbye and Sarah experienced a moment of sadness for all the years she and Serena had missed. But they had each other now and that's what

She held

Printed in the U.S.A.
Publisher acknowledges the copyright holder of the excerpt from this individual work as follows:
THE RIGHT WOMAN Copyright © 2004 by Linda Warren. All rights reserved.
® and ™ are trademarks owned and used by the trademark owner and/or its licensee.

The Harlequin Reader Service™ — Here's How It Works:

Accepting your 2 free Harlequin Presents® larger print books and gift places you under no obligation to buy anything. You may keep the books and gift and return the shipping statement marked "cancel." If you do not cancel, about a month later we'll send you 6 additional Harlequin Presents larger print books and bill you just $4.05 each in the U.S., or $4.72 each in Canada, plus 25¢ shipping & handling per book and applicable taxes if any.* That's the complete price and — compared to cover prices of $4.75 each in the U.S. and $5.50 each in Canada — it's quite a bargain! You may cancel at any time, but if you choose to continue, every month we'll send you 6 more books, which you may either purchase at the discount price or return to us and cancel your subscription.

*Terms and prices subject to change without notice. Sales tax applicable in N.Y. Canadian residents will be charged applicable provincial taxes and GST.

"What do you mean?" Devon's hands fisted at his sides.

"He's like a frat boy in a man's life, picking up women just for the sex." Her breath clouded a small patch of glass as she spoke, fogging a circle just beyond her lips. "He wrote me off before we had drinks because he perceived my sexual interest to be a couple steps behind my relationship interest, which may not necessarily have been true, but which I find a very tacky accusation. And all the while he was dismissing me, I think he might have been flirting with our waitress."

The hint of bitterness…no, hurt…in her voice had Devon closing the last couple of inches between them to slide his hands around her waist. He didn't know what this week held for them besides a sexual dynamic he couldn't ignore, but he damn well wanted to give Jenny whatever he could during their time together. She possessed strength and courage. Drive and determination. And he admired all those qualities even if this week was all they would ever share. She deserved more than a man who carried a lot of baggage about her phobia. She deserved someone who would put her first.

"Brady is an idiot if he looked at any other woman while you were sitting across the table from him." Hell, Devon couldn't take his eyes off her any time they were in the same room. "When I first saw you in your suite the other night, walking out of the bedroom with those garters hugging your thighs…" just thinking about it made his temperature spike and his hands squeeze her waist tighter "…I figured I must have hit some kind of cosmic jackpot to get so lucky."

Figuring he'd learned all he could about Brady's relationship with Jenny anyhow, Devon was only too glad to change the subject. Even more glad to have an excuse to touch her. He'd get to the bottom of the Brady debacle tomorrow when Jenny was safely occupied with her seminars and wouldn't care about a stupid power struggle between Brady and him which amounted to no more than a very public pissing contest.

Grazing her hip, he savored the feel of her through the thin fabric of her dress. Right up until she locked his wrist in a surprisingly strong grip.

"Believe me, my ego appreciates your assessment and flattery might get you everywhere on any other day, but right now I want to know what's going on between you and Dave Brady to make you think he would follow us."

JENNY COULDN'T LET him touch her or she'd lose every bit of focus. The man's hands could set fire to her best intentions, turning her willpower to ash and her body into a writhing mass of need. No way would she let him rest so much as a pinkie finger on her until she got some answers.

"I hate to drag you into this—"

"I'm already in. This guy played me for a sucker when he gave me the wrong e-mail address, Dev. Lucky for us his ploy had beaucoup benefits, but it could have been extremely embarrassing." Devastating, even. At least from her point of view. She had enough crap to cope with in her head without people trying to screw her up even more.

When Devon didn't say anything for a long moment, she pushed harder.

"The guy helped himself to a free show by spying on us in the racquetball court and who knows how much he saw. Don't you think I deserve the satisfaction of knowing why?"

She turned to face him, although it was difficult to look away from the view out his sliding glass door. The lights were on and the drapes were open in a handful of rooms that let her take an intimate glance into people's private lives.

Something about that wide-angle perspective of other people's worlds soothed the agoraphobic in her, desensitizing her in some small way to the handful of settings that she could see. It wasn't as effective as being in all those different places and experiencing them firsthand, but this method helped, too.

And, she had to admit, there might be a small voyeurism factor that played into her interest.

"As for what Brady hoped to accomplish by playing Peeping Tom, I don't really know. Honestly." Devon shrugged, the open collar of his shirt gaping a little more with the movement and making her itch to undress him. "Maybe he's a stone-cold pervert among his other shortcomings, but the reason I guessed he might be following me is because I'm angling to dispute his new position as head of Shore Engineers. I've been talking to members of the board about it and I wondered if he could have somehow gotten wind of my efforts."

"He's an engineer, not a private investigator." Jenny couldn't make the pieces fit in her head, hoping Devon wouldn't think that a smidge of voyeurism was perverted. "Doesn't that sound a little bit cloak-and-dagger for boardroom politics?"

"Bet it makes you happy you're self-employed, doesn't it?" He jammed his fists in his pockets and leaned a shoulder against the door.

"Yes, but don't change the subject." A movement out the window caught her eye, a flash of naked limbs in a hotel room across the courtyard two floors down. The angle of the window and a low hanging window treatment made it impossible to see the couple's whole bodies, but their naked hips and thighs were in plain view. Both *female* naked hips and thighs, interestingly enough. How could Devon not find the view intriguing? "There must be something disreputable or dishonorable about Dave Brady to make you suspect him of invading your privacy and shadowing you even after you gave your notice to leave his company."

Jenny watched the couple's legs twine, one woman's thigh lifting to wrap around the other woman's hip. She caught a glimpse of bright pink toenails and a tattoo of a butterfly before Devon's hand ventured back to her waist to draw her closer.

"I told you, I don't like him. His own father didn't trust him. Brady never cared about his old man's business until the guy kicked the bucket and I can't help but think his son saw a way to finally get his hands on Dad's assets." He lowered his voice, slowly walking his fingers down her thigh. "It's interesting what you can see from here, isn't it?"

"Changing the subject again?" She smiled at his astute observation, although perhaps men had built-in radar for chick-on-chick encounters. The view from Devon's suite had gained momentum as the women gently wrestled, vying for dominance. Lean muscles flexed and stretched. Fingers crept over one another's skin to cover new ground.

"No, just following your lead." He hiked the material up until he had a fistful of silky fabric, her bright blue satin panties exposed for his viewing pleasure. And touching pleasure. Even now, he ran a stray finger over the curve of her rump. "And you seem to be enjoying the parade of feminine flesh across the way."

"No harm in a little visual pleasure, is there? I think a little outside stimulation offers extra incentive to get naked sometimes." To prove her point, she hooked a finger in Devon's belt and reeled him closer. "But while the frolicking females across the way have great bods, I'd rather get a handful of hot, hard he-man."

She felt his abs tense beneath her finger, his erection rising to the occasion since she'd made it the star of the conversation.

"Looks like the ladies across the way agree." Devon cupped her bottom, lifted her, to situate her hips right up against his.

Curious, Jenny turned to peer out the window in time to see a pair of masculine legs in silky black boxers walk into the bedroom of the kissing girls. The anonymous man came up behind one of the women, bending her over the bed and rubbing himself against her while the other female with waist-length red hair and a tattoo near her panty line sidled back as if to watch the action.

Jenny might have watched longer if not for the heat of Devon's body burning through her clothes, demanding her response.

"Interesting, but not nearly as much fun as what we're going to have." She reached for the curtains, ready for the privacy to have her way with him.

"Wait." Devon blocked her wrist, preventing her from closing the drapes. "Holy crap."

Puzzled, Jenny followed his gaze to the view below. The tattooed redhead had cocked her arm back as if to strike the woman bent over the bed with a submissive smile on her face—at the same moment as the man in silk boxers drew their blinds shut.

9

"I NEVER GUESSED I'd be a person with paranoid tendencies, but I've gotta say the thought of people striking each other as a way of getting their kicks sort of freaks me out." Devon yanked the curtains closed for her as he spoke, but even with two sets of blinds between them and the trio of sexual adventurers across the courtyard, the image from the other window remained burned in Jenny's mind.

"Lucky for you there are seminars for paranoid people by the dozen this week." She refused to let the erotic antics of total strangers ruin this night for her when she only had limited time with Devon left. The conference ran for six days—Monday to Saturday— and even though she didn't plan to drive home until Sunday morning, she didn't think she'd see Devon again after Saturday. That gave her three more nights with him after tonight—not enough time to justify borrowing trouble from other people's lives. "Want me to see if I can sign you up for your own personalized self-help schedule?"

She backed him away from the sliding glass

door toward his bedroom, her hand still hooked around his belt.

"Doesn't the thought of that lady raising her hand against her uh...friend...make you want to run down there and save the object of her disciplinary tactics?" Devon speared a hand through his hair before he crushed her to him in a hard embrace.

"That's some people's idea of fun. Besides, didn't you notice the friend was smiling like she loved every minute of it?" She inhaled the scent of him, the combination of starch in his shirt and aftershave a familiar fragrance that would forever jump-start her libido. "Remember, there are a lot of people attending the self-help conference this weekend who might have sexual addictions or unusual preferences—nymphomaniacs, erotomaniacs, you name it."

"Sadists?"

"God, I hope not." She shuddered, still hoping they could recover the sizzle and spark their touches had ignited earlier. "I like to think anybody who wants to seek self-help and a supportive network of peers would try hard not to hurt anyone else who suffered from related afflictions, wouldn't you?"

"Maybe." Devon's whole body remained tense as he held her, clearly torn between a need to address the playful violence they'd witnessed across the way and his own desire to pick up where they'd left off. "But who's to say there aren't even more twisted individuals who seek out this kind of venue to prey upon their peers?"

A scary thought.

"But what would you have us do? Call hotel security so we can admit we were spying on a private encounter that didn't concern us?" She released him, freeing herself from his strong hold. She had the feeling her hopes for another delectable romp in bed with Devon had been well and truly squashed.

"Is it so bad to be a concerned citizen?"

"I learned how to fight off paranoid tendencies a long time ago watching out for my mother. And believe me, it's easy to jump to the scariest conclusions when you're hanging out with a woman who's always convinced you're going to die of a long and painful illness every time you catch the sniffles. But that kind of negative thinking is the surest path to sickness—emotional or mental or physical."

"Damn, Jen, that redhead was winding up to smack someone down there. She sure didn't look like she was playing to me."

"But nobody's body language looked particularly unhappy, did it? Those chicks were making out five minutes prior." She couldn't buy trouble. Not when she'd come so far from those scary days of worrying about her mother, about her own mental health, every night. "Did you know that you make your whole body vulnerable to physical sickness when you let your mind play tricks on you? That's why I never snicker at all the self-help stuff, goofy though some of it might sound. I know firsthand that the power of positive thinking has quite possibly saved me from losing my mind."

"Shit." Devon let out a breath and gave an abrupt nod, but the stern set to his features didn't make him look all that convinced. "I can see the point, but I don't necessarily like it. Bottom line, what goes on behind closed doors is none of my business."

"Although it sure busted the mood in a hurry, didn't it?" Jenny mourned the loss of the sexual adrenaline that had her on edge in the racquetball court and again at the window a few moments ago watching the free show across the courtyard before things ventured into a potentially frightening dimension.

Definitely *not* sexy in her book, but then, turn-ons were majorly subjective.

Ask any Playmate of the month.

"So what do you say we get a change of scenery to forget about the crazy threesome and think about what you'd like to do for fun tonight instead?" He skimmed a light touch up the back of her forearm, eliciting a shiver of anticipation. "I've been thinking I could use some tips on kicking back and living the life of luxury from an expert."

"Is that so?" She had Devon pegged for a worka-holic, so that didn't surprise her one bit. "I thought you loved your work even if you don't like the actual job because of David."

"I'm crazy about the work, but a man can't bury himself in his career just because it's fun. Everybody's got to come up for air once in a while."

"In that case, we can do each other a favor." She liked the sound of that. She'd be helping Devon for a change and not just the other way around. "You venture out with me to unexplored terrain—a place of my choice—and I'll make sure the experience is totally self-indulgent for you."

"Deal." He scooped his room key off the counter near the entrance to his suite and stuffed it in his wallet. "Where should we go?"

"I've got to get ready first." Heading for the door, she hoped Devon wouldn't reject her next idea for a desensitization exercise. "You don't mind if we don't get much sleep tonight, do you?"

"Hell, I'm banking on no sleep." He lined up the papers on the kitchen counter into neat rows, not a single sheaf amiss. "If this night is half as much fun as the last two, I'll be smiling all damn day tomorrow."

Jenny glanced at the digital clock blinking in a red LCD display above the sleek black stovetop. "It's 11:45 now. Why don't I meet you in the lobby just past midnight?"

"The lobby?" His eyebrows lifted in unison.

"Yes." Tugging open the door, she started a list in her head of things to bring, the hum of anticipation and barely leashed sexual energy buzzing in her veins. "And if it's not too much trouble, could you bring the keys to your vehicle?"

TWO HOURS LATER, Devon parked his pickup truck in front of the deserted boardwalk in Seaside Heights, a resort town whose population of three thousand swelled to ten times that many in the summertime. The wind whipped off the waves, rolling up the expanse of shore to blow specks of sand in their faces while the carnival rides loomed as dark shadows in the distance. The amusements stretched longer here than on the Steel Pier, over two miles of slides and rides, arcade games standing shoulder to shoulder with gambling parlors, tattoo dens and booths for henna art.

"So this is home sweet home for you?" Devon had been surprised and oddly pleased when Jenny confided their destination tonight. She wanted to bring him to her home turf? Surely that meant she was starting to trust him. Care about him?

An unexpected thought.

"I live a couple of miles south of here, actually." She pointed the way, her cashmere blanket that she'd filched from her hotel room cloaking her shoulders like a cape. She'd dragged a big bag with her, too, a canvas tote full of things that clanked when she walked, but which she'd refused to let him carry. Apparently the bag contained some of his surprises for the night.

"Must be nice. Can you see the water?"

"Actually, I can see this exact stretch of board-walk from my apartment window, and when the wind is blowing just right I hear the screams from the mini roller coaster and the bells from the strong-man games where people try to win a bear by wielding a big hammer."

The thought of her sitting alone in her apartment while so much excitement brewed nearby gave Devon a hollow feeling in his chest—the same kind of ache he'd known as a kid staring down at performers trying to make a buck on the streets of South Philly twenty years ago.

"And you've never been down here?" He couldn't stifle a flare of resentment toward her mother for not getting her act together enough to give Jenny a few normal childhood memories.

"My dad brought me to the beach a couple of times before he gave up on my mom and quit visiting us altogether." She hugged the blanket more tightly around her. "But I always felt too guilty about leaving my mom—even as a very young kid—to enjoy the boardwalk experience. I think he brought me here just to worry my mother, in fact, because he knew she'd never go here when the lights and the noise and all the people would freak her out."

"Pretty sad when the adults are the ones playing games when they split." Devon hit the remote to lock his truck and then pocketed the keys so he could sling an arm around Jenny's shoulders, and maybe pry his hand under the strap of her tote bag to share a little of the weight.

"I bet it's more common than we'd like to think, but I'm sure my mother didn't make it easy on my father either." She shrugged, the motion subtle but discernible since he had her tucked under his arm as they started toward the boardwalk lit only by a handful of streetlights at two in the morning. "So I've been down here, just not enough to plant the place in my head as comfortable terrain. For that matter, I think those guilty trips I made with my father only cemented it in my mind as a spot I shouldn't venture to."

"Not after tonight, I hope." He liked her idea of desensitization since it appealed to the engineer side of his brain with a definite timetable for success. Still, the role she wanted him to play was integral and already he feared failing her.

Not tonight, necessarily, because he really wanted to be with her.

But how would he fit into her life and her plans after this week when they lived in different cities with very different lifestyles and expectations? Would she forget all about her hopes for beating her phobia once the seminar was over? He couldn't understand why such a strong, capable woman had allowed her fears to rule her life for so long already.

"It smells like popcorn even in winter." She

breathed deep as they neared the strip, inciting Devon to do the same.

"And cotton candy." Seaside Heights was nirvana in his book with the parade of rides and games and even an overhead sky ride to take visitors from one end of the boardwalk to the other.

A rope closed off the top of the stairs to the boardwalk but Devon easily climbed over it and then helped Jenny do the same. The tote bag she carried bumped his leg, reminding him she had an ulterior motive for bringing him here that didn't involve desensitization.

One that involved fun. Relaxation.

Self-indulgence.

The possibilities tantalized him, especially with the feel of her hand in his as she led him deeper onto the planked walkway along the beach, skirting around the kiddie rides toward the giant Ferris wheel and the looming needle structure that could only be the Tower of Fear.

Having worked on thrill rides all along the eastern seaboard, Devon had heard of this 225-foot drop ride, but he'd never visited the Funtown Pier that served as its home. Everything was dark and closed down for the night, possibly for the season, but the giant rides perched on the Atlantic Ocean had to be spectacular in the daytime when they were lit and running.

"This puts the Steel Pier to shame." He drew her closer under his arm as he spotted a group of teens prowling the deserted boardwalk.

"Only if you're an adrenaline junkie." She peered up at the tower ride, their steps slowing as they neared the monstrous attraction. "Historical purists would claim the Steel Pier has a far more lofty heritage with all the teen idols that played there when it was a concert venue."

"And what about you, Ms. Moore?" He dropped his chin on the top of her head, allowing himself a feel of her silky hair against his jaw. "Which appeals to you?"

"Well, this one is home." Her words drifted upward along with her gaze. "I don't know that I'll ever conquer the tower, but I'd like to think I could stroll through here in the daylight now that I've seen it all up close and personal while it's empty."

His arms cinched around her waist and he wondered if he'd ever have the chance to walk by her side down this pier again, or would she make that trek on her own?

Then again, maybe now that she was ready to tackle the world newly desensitized she would meet someone else who would welcome the chance to hold her the way Devon was right now. A chilling thought that didn't have a thing to do with the March wind blowing off the waves.

"Maybe you could give me a shout next time you want to tackle the pier and I could take a ride over here. Whether I'm back in Philly or in Wildwood working with Shore, this place isn't all that far away."

He didn't know where the proposition came from exactly. Maybe a stray protective urge brought on by the sexual power play they'd witnessed back in Atlantic City.

Or maybe his impromptu suggestion didn't have a thing to do with that, and only meant he resented the idea of anyone else touching Jenny. If she'd let him be a part of her life, he could provide all the thrills she'd ever need.

"Meaning you think we could see each other after this week? So I could run the risk of disappointing you all over again if I couldn't find the courage to battle my phobia that particular day?" She shook her head as she moved out of the circle of his arms. "I'd rather we end this thing on a more upbeat note than me hyperventilating inside my apartment and you banging your head against the wall because you can't handle the stress."

Well damn.

Her accusation stung enough that he had to ask himself if perhaps she had a point. Would he be able to handle that kind of setback? He honestly didn't know.

But he hadn't realized how much he liked the idea of seeing her again after this week until she shot it down so fast. Disappointment squeezed him hard even as he reassessed his tactical approach with her.

"I don't think it would be like that." He wanted to say outright that it wouldn't, but he'd never been the kind of guy to give his word unless he knew for sure he could keep it. He swiped away a strand of her hair blowing across her jaw in the relentless wind. "But I respect that you need to decide that for yourself."

"I just think it would be better to enjoy the here and now than to speculate about a future that seems destined to relegate this week to a one-time fling." She hitched her canvas tote higher on her shoulder and nodded toward the main boardwalk a little way up the pier. "Why don't we head down there and I'll share my surprise for you?"

Devon told himself he was a grown man and damn well mature enough to enjoy this night with Jenny despite her dismal take on any sort of future. But even as he mustered a halfhearted nod, he couldn't shake the feeling that walking away from her after Saturday would be a big mistake.

For *both* of them.

He just had to figure out how to convince Jenny she needed him as much as he'd begun to fear he needed her.

JENNY WASN'T SURE how to read Devon's long silence as they sat under the protective shelter of the board-walk an hour later, the remnants of their predawn feast strewn over the beach blanket that doubled as a canvas tote with a bit of ingenious rolling. She'd brought along all the little luxuries from her De-Luxe catalog that she thought Devon would get a kick out of, from the miniature hurricane lamp with scented oil lighting their nocturnal picnic to the silk and angora lap throw they shared as defense against the wind.

She hadn't had time to whip up a gourmet meal, but she'd raided the hotel minibar in her suite and rustled up a pretty good facsimile with an M&M's appetizer and a main course of peanuts, oatmeal cookies and apples. But she'd saved the best for last—the champagne cocktails served with raspberries filched from the lobby bar on their way out the front door.

Now, Jenny reached to raise the wick on the hurricane lamp enough to brighten the glow around their beach blanket so she could see Devon's face. His profile made her catch her breath, his chiseled jaw and sculpted cheekbones rendered all the more stark and male in the shadows of their hideaway beneath the planked walkway overhead.

"So what do you think?" She turned the wick back down to its shorter height, cooling the lamp's glow to a dull flicker. "Do you feel appropriately spoiled now that you've indulged in a shoreside party after hours with all the bells and whistles?"

"You throw a hell of a shindig, I'll grant you that." He helped her clear off the empty wrappers and tiny champagne bottles from the minibar, tucking everything into a plastic laundry bag from the hotel until their tote could be resurrected from the beach blanket. "But I have to admit that I've still got one burning question about your hostess qualifications."

"Mmm?" She propped an elbow on the pink angora throw pillow she'd brought along for good measure. "And what question is that?"

"Do you provide any after-dinner entertainment at your parties or am I going to have to think of something on my own?"

"I'm not the kind of woman who puts herself on center stage even on a good day, so I'm definitely not providing any entertainment." She stared up at the Tower of Fear and patted herself on the back for having made it this far. "I consider it a triumph that I made it to the middle of a venue that's normally packed full of people every summer and I didn't freak out. Maybe now I can come back here when there aren't too many people early in the season. Work myself back up to facing bigger crowds."

Devon leaned back on an elbow beside her, his long, denim clad legs stretched out in front of him. She could feel the warmth of his presence through her wool jacket, the heat of him chasing away the chill of sand beneath their blanket and the misty spray wafting off wind-tossed water.

"So now that you've taken care of the dinner and the desensitizing thing, I guess it's up to me to provide the post-meal diversion. Maybe make a memory to keep you too hot and bothered to get freaked out next time you come down to the boardwalk." He unbuttoned her coat with slow, deliberate fingers, taking care to uncover as little of her as possible when he slid his palm beneath the wool. "Any suggestions for what would amuse you?"

Jenny wanted to answer, her brain firing off steamy suggestions at an alarming rate, but Devon's sure, slow touches up her rib cage to tease the underside of her breast through the fabric of her dress left her tongue-tied.

She'd thought about changing into pants for the trek to the beach, but ended up throwing on a second silk slip to keep the wind out of her dress, appreciating the warmth conservation factor of having her legs together. And, of course, it had occurred to her that a dress offered sensual access opportunities she wouldn't have with pants.

Besides, tonight she'd come prepared for the weather with their choice of luxurious fabrics to toss over them for warmth.

"Come on, Jen," Devon's voice urged in her ear as her eyelids slid closed. "Tell me how you want me to please you."

He eased her back all the way against the beach blanket, her head resting on the pillow while he remained propped above her as they shared body heat. They were sheltered from most of the wind here, their nook under the boardwalk a private haven now that even the pack of prowling teens had long sought their beds for the night.

"I've been around you enough to know you don't need instructions," she whispered back, dragging her bare foot up the back of his pants leg, her hem gliding up her thigh to expose more of her skin.

"But just because I have the tools doesn't mean I'm the best man for any job." His fingers fanned out over the top of her breast, the heat of him penetrating her dress and causing her skin to tighten and tingle. "Look at it like an engineering project. I get the best results when I share my expertise with my client's needs. When we both weigh in on how the project should unfold, we get the best possible results."

"Really?" She shifted under his stilled fingers, putting his touch where she needed it, right at the center of her breast. "What if I tell you that I put implicit trust in your ability to deliver the final product?"

He scraped away her coat lapels and the blanket to expose more of her breast and then bent to exhale a hot breath over the lightweight fabric.

"Then I'd be flattered but I'd still ask you for a little guidance while I discover the fine line between what makes you hot and bothered and what makes you moan so loud it brings security sprinting down here to see what's wrong."

Jenny's breath caught in her throat, the image of getting so carried away with sex sending a tremor of anticipation through her thighs to vibrate ever so subtly between her legs.

Wrapping her arms around Devon's shoulders she drew him closer and rocked her hips hard against his.

"In that case, you can start off by hiking up my dress and taking a peek at the one last surprise I have in store for you."

10

THE WOMAN blew his mind.

At least, Devon told himself that had to be what was happening right now since he couldn't think, couldn't speak, couldn't do anything but gawk at Jenny's choice of lingerie as he flung aside the dress she'd been wearing. She must have changed when she went to her suite back at the hotel, because the bright blue panties she'd worn earlier had been exchanged for a black lace outfit covering her from breasts to hips with a keyhole cutout to showcase a mouthwatering expanse of cleavage.

Panels of fabric stretched taut over her ribs and abs, molding her curvy shape into more exaggerated lines, cinching her waist and drawing his eye to the round defiance of hips that refused to be constrained. Another cutout nestled just above her pubic bone in the shape of two cherries, outlined by bright red embroidery easily visible in the light of the hurricane lamp.

"What's the matter?" She tipped up his chin with one finger to look her in the eye. "You don't like my surprises?"

"I'm crazy about your surprises." His voice scratched over his suddenly dry throat, the scent of sea air and warm woman filling his nostrils. "If I wasn't paralyzed by lust, I'd be turning cartwheels."

She smothered a laugh, apparently having no idea he was dead serious. He'd never had a woman rob him of so many brain cells.

"Is that so?" She drew the cashmere blanket up higher on his shoulders in their boardwalk haven, effectively covering them both since he still lay half on top of her. "How about you just turn me on instead?"

Hunger for her roared inside him, demanding release.

"Ask and you shall receive." He tugged on the strap of her outfit, peeling a satin ribbon off one shoulder.

She arched her back at just that small contact, a satisfied hum purring in her throat as he bent to taste her shoulder and the soft hollow beneath her collarbone. The needy sound goaded him on, making it impossible for him to plan the ultimate seduction with engineering precision.

"Are you warm enough?" His hands conformed to black lace and womanly curves and he ached to bury himself inside her, but he needed to make sure she was okay with doing this now. Here.

Outdoors in March, for crying out loud.

"I'm burning up." She nudged his hand lower on her hip, guiding him toward the cutout in the shape of cherries. "See for yourself."

His finger grazed the hot silk of her skin through the lace, his touch wrenching another low moan from her throat. He could grow addicted to that sound, addicted to *her.*

He kissed her hard, savoring the raspberry flavor that lingered on her lips. His fingers trailed lower over her hip to the juncture of her thighs where he discovered even more heat and—much to his delight—tiny covered snaps for easy access. Sand shifting under the blanket beneath them, he positioned himself over her as he released the fasteners.

He might have regretted the haste except that Jenny moved with even more speed, her fingers flicking open his fly to stroke him. Eyes rolling back in his head at the feel of her soft hands gliding over him, Devon promised himself he wouldn't let Jenny walk out of his life until he'd had a chance to take his time. How long could this fevered frenzy last between two people anyway?

Ducking to capture her nipple in his mouth, he admired the way the light from a faraway streetlamp slanted through the slats in the boardwalk overhead to illuminate a thin line down her chest to point at her hip. He followed the line with his finger as he drew her deep in his mouth and rolled the tender flesh along his teeth.

She must have reached for a condom from her bag of tricks at some point because she held him steady to sheathe him.

"They're vanilla flavored." She blinked up at him in the dim glow from the hurricane lamp that had ended up down by their feet. "Want me to take a taste to test them out?"

His cock bobbed in her hand in answer, but Devon couldn't let her make an attempt here with the board-walk overhead.

"We'd better stay low," he warned, imprisoning her wrists when her hands brought him too close to release. "You'll just have to take the manufacturer's word for it that they're vanilla flavored."

She stretched beneath him, her breasts lifting to give him an even more tempting, close-up view.

"Okay, but I can't wait longer." She raised her hips, nudging him where she wanted him. "I've been on edge ever since the racquetball court and I'm going to explode if I don't get—"

He entered her in one long, slow thrust. Her breath caught. Held. Her nails scratched his back harder than he would have expected, but as he looked down into her face he guessed she didn't have any idea what she was doing.

That same tide of powerful sensation swept over him, threatening to pull him under, but he grounded himself in the feel of the sand under his right knee where he'd slipped off the beach blanket. The grains rubbed into his skin, a welcome counterpoint to Jenny's tight heat gripping him, squeezing, making him lose his mind. But he wanted to drive her crazy, damn it, not the other way around. He needed to make her understand they could never get enough of each other in just one week.

Withdrawing from her until only the head of his erection teased her, he ground his teeth and gathered enough restraint to ease out the rest of the way.

Her helpless mewl of frustration dissolved into a satisfied sigh as he worked his way south, kissing, licking and nipping down her body to the slick folds between her thighs. He spread her wide, swirling his tongue over the slick center of her until her breath grew shallow and her back bowed.

Only then did he make his way up her body to cover her. He drove into her again and again, taking all she had to give and more, urging her higher whenever she stilled, teetering on the verge of release. He wanted to go down in flames with her tonight, to experience the ultimate fusion of mutual fulfillment.

And he loomed so close now. Could almost taste the mind-blowing finish that awaited him. Just before it took him, he changed his angle over top of her so he could graze her clit with each stroke. She bucked beneath him, clutched his shoulders, her fingers digging into his skin while her thighs went taut.

His release hammered through him the same moment she cried out with her own. Their bodies sealed together with damp sweat, their scents mingling along with their shouts. Devon couldn't move afterward as he held her while she trembled with aftershocks, his arms dead weight since he'd poured all of himself into her.

Once she'd quieted beneath him, he collapsed beside her, spent.

"I can't get enough of you." He hoped his words were intelligible despite the weary delivery into her hair. But he'd grown addicted to her thirst for adventure and he couldn't imagine ever tiring of what they shared.

"Lucky for you, I seem to have an insatiable appetite where you're concerned, too." She ducked her head into his chest.

They were quiet for six incoming rushes of the tide as Devon timed his breathing to mirror the lazy roll of waves in an effort to get his heart rate back under control.

"Can I ask you something?"

"Shoot."

"You said you had a reason for sprinting out of my hotel suite that first morning. I wasn't sure I wanted to know it last night, but by now, I'm kind of curious." Her fingers traced slow, deliberate patterns on his chest. "Is the offer still open for you to clue me in?"

Devon sucked in a bracing breath, his attempt to relax with the soothing roll of the tide no longer an option if Jenny wanted a peek in his head. He owed her an explanation but that didn't make him any more eager to talk about the past. He had a solid relation-

ship with his mother now, he'd just never been a su-
persentimental guy. Whatever he dredged up to share
with Jenny would probably only raise more questions
in her head than it answered for her.

"Of course." He skimmed a hand along her arm
to rest on her hip, allowing himself the pleasure of
her naked skin as long as he was baring a piece of
his soul. "I just got a little spooked when you said
you didn't leave the house much because I grew up
with a housebound parent. My mom and dad had a
car accident that killed my father and left my mother
paralyzed from the waist down when I was six."

Lifting her head to look at him, Jenny made a
little gulping, gasping noise. A surprised yelp that she
sort of stifled with the back of her hand to her lips.

"I never thought— I'm so sorry, Devon. I wondered why you left, but it never occurred to me you'd
have such a direct experience with being tied to the
house."

"It's okay. I've lived with the way that accident
changed my whole world for a long time. But my
mom wasn't bed-bound or anything, she just refused
to venture out into the world with her wheelchair. She
always resented it." Once he was older—hell, even
by the time he was eight—he'd tried to get her to
attend church, to go out for ice cream, to do anything,
but she wouldn't budge.

And worse, sometimes she'd cried. Eventually it
seemed too selfish for him to push her to go any-

where and he'd done what he could to bring the world home to her.

"She probably associated her injury with the loss of her husband, so maybe she didn't want to accept her physical challenges." Jenny shook her head in mute sympathy, her eyes shiny with compassion for a woman she'd never met. "How hard for her. And you."

He preferred not to think about the effect his mother's choices had on his life. He'd moved on even if she hadn't, although a small part of him had always cringed with guilt for enjoying life when she couldn't. Wouldn't. He didn't know which.

"I had friends. I went places eventually. My eighth grade class went to an amusement park at the end of the school year and that's where I discovered roller coasters."

"And you've been hooked ever since?" She smiled, bending her head to brush a kiss along his neck.

"I remember being so surprised that some kids were really blasé about being there because their parents took them all the time. I swore I'd never get jaded about the thrills in life the way they were, so I guess yeah, I discovered how to have fun that summer." And another thought occurred to him as he remembered those spoiled kids who didn't care about the rides anymore. "Maybe that's why I've never gotten along with Dave Brady. He had so much handed to him that he can't even appreciate what's in front of him."

The sound of the waves carried him back to the

present, back to the conversation with Jenny and making him realize she wasn't asking any more questions about his past or his reason for walking out that first morning. Instead, she simply stroked her fingers through his hair, down the back of his neck.

"Anyway, just the thought of being with someone who couldn't go outside made me tear out your door the other day, but I realized pretty quickly afterward that your phobia isn't anything like my mother's refusal to leave the house. I'm sorry I panicked. You deserved a better morning-after than that."

"You're very much forgiven." Her thumb followed the ridge of his cheekbone, skimming lower to graze his mouth. "Thank you for telling me."

Her simple words and easy forgiveness made him think it hadn't been so hard baring a little soul, even if he was relieved to have it over with. But then, Jenny seemed to surprise him at every turn.

When a gust of wind kicked up on the beach he reached to tuck her head under his arm to protect her from any stray sand squalls. His foot kicked the miniature hurricane lamp, knocking the glass sideways into the sand so that the flame went out.

"I'll buy you a new one if I broke it."

For now, he just wanted the chance to hold her for a little while as the sound of the waves rolling onto the beach lulled him, helping him forget everything he'd left behind in Atlantic City. Jenny had told him she thought sexual distraction might be her ticket out of agoraphobia, but Devon had never suspected it could obliterate some of his problems, too.

He'd always thought he and Lori were missing out on a lot more than sex with her refusal to sleep with him, but since he was a guy—and worse, an engineer—he didn't have the sensitivity quotient to explain what that "more" might be. He still couldn't put a name to that form of intimacy. But he knew damn sure this sense of connection he felt to Jenny right now…well, this was *it*.

SHE WOULD NOT say she was afraid of the dark after Devon had just shared such an intimate sliver of his past—of him—with her.

He was such an amazing guy. And he obviously loved his mother even if she had robbed her son of *both* parents when that accident had only taken one of them.

Jenny lay perfectly still beside him in the teeny, tiny shaft of light streaming down between the planks of the boardwalk overhead. To scramble around the blankets in an attempt to relight the hurricane lamp would only make her look neurotic. Which she wasn't—she'd once taken the time to secure a certified psychiatrist's professional opinion on the matter for her own peace of mind. But somehow her agoraphobia intensified when she was not only in a new place, but a new place in the dark.

Where she couldn't possibly see what unforeseen threats lurked nearby.

She hated it that she couldn't simply revel in the afterglow of shared confidences and amazing sex with a man she'd only get to be around for a few more days. But already the tightness gripped her chest, making her wonder what potential dangers might prowl in the shadows nearby.

Or who.

"Want to go to my place?" Jenny bolted upright, seizing on the first viable excuse that came to mind without making her look like a basket case. She slid her dress over her head and stuffed her undergarments into her purse. No need to struggle with straps and hooks in the dark.

"Now?" Devon stroked her spine, his broad hands spanning half her back and diffusing some of the tension as she felt around the ground to gather up his clothes and their coats.

"It's only a couple of miles from here." And it would be safe. Familiar. Well-lit. "You have to admit I've been stretching my boundaries an awful lot this week, and going home to my own bed to sleep for a few hours could be my reward for working my butt off at this desensitizing thing."

Already she scooped up their nighttime picnic items, separating M&M's wrappers and empty champagne bottles from the things she needed to repack. Willing her hands to slow down, she breathed deep to chase away the pressure in her chest.

She would beat this phobia if it killed her. And

after she'd pummeled her old fears into oblivion, she'd take her company public and soar to new levels of business success.

Too bad she'd be all alone when she finally reached that level of achievement.

And didn't self-realization jab you at the most inconvenient times? Resenting the wet blanket intrusion on her mental pep talk, she startled when Devon suddenly took her hands, folding them inside his and forcing her to be still.

"You definitely deserve to touch home base for a few hours before we head back. Besides, it's four in the morning—bedtime even for night owls." He released her fingers with a lingering kiss and lifted his shirt from her lap. "Are you okay?"

"Great." She knew she'd answered too fast. Without thought. And she owed him better than that after what they'd just shared. "Just a little spooked about the public display of affection now that our light is out. Silly, really, since anyone passing by would have been able to see us better when the lamp was still lit, yet now that it's so dark, I'm battling a smidge of paranoia about someone seeing us."

"That's not paranoid." The rustling sounds on the other side of the beach blanket made her think he was finishing getting dressed. "I worried about that a little when our clothes first started coming off, but I was careful to keep you covered with the blanket. And then

I got too out of control to worry anymore, although I did continue to monitor the blanket pretty well."

The tension in her lungs eased at the same time her heart warmed at his words.

"You don't think I'm paranoid?"

"I think you're smart to worry. Jesus, Jen, we're out here in the middle of nowhere getting naked. Now *that* might be crazy, but I'm right there with you pleading insanity to that one."

Rising out of their boardwalk hideaway, Jenny realized she could see a little better now that her eyes adjusted to less light along the shore. Plus the street-lamp down the walkway was now in plain view, even if it loomed far in the distance.

As Devon meticulously rolled her beach blanket back into its tote capacity, she hugged her arms around herself against the wind and told herself that it shouldn't mean so much to her that Devon didn't think she was being unreasonable.

Earlier tonight he'd even said he admired the way she was trying to battle her issues. But even while she tried not to let those words matter, in her heart she knew it was already too late to warn herself away from Devon Baines.

Unfortunately, she *was* crazy.

About him.

And after one more night in his arms, she needed to figure out how she would deal with the fact that she couldn't allow herself to grow any more attached to him. She'd worked too hard to smooth out the perpetual drama that her mother had made of the world. Jenny took joy in the regular routine of her business, the calm approach to her life. So it wouldn't be fair to torture herself with loving a man who wanted his life to be one big roller coaster ride.

SWEAT DRENCHING her body, Jenny woke up in a panic, her dream of being perched at the top of the Tower of Fear with Devon urging her to try the ride still vivid in her mind.

Her bedroom was flooded with light, just the way she liked it. Her curtains were drawn but she always chose filmy materials that allowed plenty of sun to filter through. She remained alone in her king-size bed, however, with the clock radio reading 9:30 a.m.

Too damn early.

Mr. Serivolo, her eagle-eyed assistant next door, would surely notice the stranger's truck in her parking spot behind the building when he went out for his morning paper if he hadn't already.

That is, if Devon was still here.

Shaking off the remnants of a dream with obvious psychological implications, Jenny wondered why she couldn't dream in more interesting and esoteric terms, like the Marc Chagall paintings De-Luxe carried in miniature note card versions. Why did her nocturnal imagination have to be so boringly literal?

Still, with the dream fading to the back of her

mind, she noticed the shower running and solved the dilemma of Devon's whereabouts. If she didn't desperately need more emotional distance from him, she would have allowed herself to simply enjoy how nice it was to be with such a clean man. An organized man. And a really, really smart man, judging by his explanation of wind resistance, turbulence and vorticity two nights ago as they sat in the Ferris wheel cart. She wasn't sure she'd ever brave a ride after that particular discussion, but she respected his enthusiasm for his work.

So much for emotional distance. Devon Baines was all she could think about.

Reaching for the TV remote, she hoped to chase off the shaky feeling left by her nightmare with the local news. She'd given herself the week off from De-Luxe, after all, and she meant to take the much-needed vacation. Mr. Serivolo knew what to do with the business and he would take care of everything.

Assuming he didn't spend too much time speculating about Devon's truck in her spot.

"You're awake." Devon emerged from her bathroom in a cloud of steam, his bare chest looking all the more brutally masculine for her pink towel draped around his narrow hips.

And wouldn't it have been nice to quit worrying about giving herself distance and just drape herself around him instead?

"Just barely." She clicked through the local channels

on the television, desperate for anything to watch besides the easy roll of Devon's hips as he stalked across her hardwood floor dotted with jute rugs.

Heart collecting speed, she was ready to toss the remote aside and topple him into bed—to hell with the inevitable heartache next week—when a sharp rap sounded on her apartment door.

Sliding out of her sheets, she stuffed her arms into the sleeves of a white terry cloth robe and made her way out of the bedroom through the living area that served as her office.

"Who is it?" She had a pretty good idea, but she'd never been able to ignore the phone or the doorbell. Her old, two-story apartment building didn't even have peepholes on the doors, but she'd always felt safe living here.

"It's Joe. What are you doing back already?" Her assistant's voice grew louder as she neared the barrier and finally wrenched it open. "There's a strange truck in your spot. I was worried."

So worried that he promptly peered over her shoulder into her apartment as if he expected a glimpse of an assailant. At seventy years old, Joe was sharp as a tack and had a keen mind for business. His advice had kept Jenny firmly in the black since her second year running De-Luxe, and while he had always been quick to credit her eye for marketable products and her production savvy with the catalog, Jenny knew his help had been instrumental to her success.

"It's my friend's truck." She normally wouldn't think twice about having Joe in for coffee while wearing her bathrobe since he was more like a favorite uncle than an employee, but since Devon lurked in the apartment nearly naked, that didn't seem like the best idea today. "We went to the beach last night and then came here to crash, but I'm heading back to the seminar in Atlantic City later today."

"You went to the beach?" Looking quite comfortable to stand in the cool gray morning and shoot the breeze, Joe leaned a shoulder into the whitewashed door frame, his dark eyes narrowing in an expression that pulled the lines on his sun-weathered face into well-used formation. "That seminar must be doing you a world of good, Jenny. I'm glad to hear it."

"Thanks. I'll call you on Sunday afternoon like we planned and we can catch up about what happened this week while I was out of the office."

"I told you I'm not talking business with you five minutes after you get home, for crying out loud. Monday will come soon enough." He rose on his tiptoes to see over her head since they were the same height. "Any chance I'll get to meet the fellow with the truck?"

"Definitely not." She peered over her shoulder, grateful that Devon hadn't wandered out of the bedroom in a towel. "We're, um, getting ready to go out."

The older man's shaggy brows lifted in surprise.

"After all the planning it took you to leave the apartment the first time, I have to say I'm mighty damn impressed that you're ready to put your feet to the fire all over again, but more power to you."

Her heart warmed, knowing Joe didn't dole out praise lightly. In business he gave his best and expected the same from her, but he wasn't one to take the time to hand out compliments unless he meant them.

"One way or another, I'm taking De-Luxe public. I figure I need to get out of the apartment if I ever want to follow through on meetings with underwriters to see what kind of backing we can secure." She'd done her homework and had talked to a few companies over the phone, but she needed to set up the meetings to push through the paperwork to take De-Luxe to the next level.

"I thought I convinced you to wait on that?" Joe shook his head. "I spent a lot of years dancing to a board of directors' tune, Jenny. You might be on your own if you're serious about calling in a bunch of strangers to run the company."

"We'll maintain creative control." She had enough savings to buy the majority shares since she wouldn't sell out her stake in the company she'd worked so hard to build. But if she didn't allow the company to grow as big as it could, to fulfill its potential, she'd always worry that she'd somehow allowed her personal issues to limit her professionally. And that she would not permit. "You'll change your mind when you see what kind of resources we gain from the influx of operating income and savvy business minds."

Or so she hoped. Joe had been her right arm from the start.

"Bah. You'll gain a whole bunch of know-it-alls trying to tell you how to do what you know best." He made a humbug gesture, waving away her attempt to lure him to her side as he straightened and took a step back. "But this guy with the truck, you make sure he treats you right, you hear?"

She nodded, less enthused about her business future without Joe at her side. Damn it, why hadn't she listened to him before when he'd tried to tell her the downside of moving to the corporate big leagues? She'd just assumed he had said those things to ease her self-imposed pressure to go public, but obviously he'd meant every word.

"I will." She tugged the tie on her bathrobe tighter, not knowing where she stood with Devon and not even sure about her business anymore, the one arena where she'd always led with confidence.

"Because you deserve the best, Jenny. Don't let any of those self-help gurus tell you anything different, you hear? You're one lady with your head screwed on straight, and there aren't too many people I can say that about these days." He pointed his finger at her like a gun and pulled the make-believe trigger of his thumb as he winked. "Have a good one."

Nodding, Jenny closed the door behind him, a jumble of thoughts whistling through her head as she made her way back to her bedroom. Following the sound of the television, she told herself that Joe didn't understand her phobia and that his generation was simply more inclined to write off mental health issues as weaknesses that could be overcome with strong will and effort. A "pull yourself up by the bootstraps" mentality.

She knew that thinking didn't make sense for some people. For a lot of people. But what if he had a point where she was concerned? Her feet slowed just outside the bedroom, Devon's words about her being one of the most sane people he knew coming back to echo what Joe said.

Was there a chance she was far more normal than she realized? And hard on the heels of that thought, she had to wonder if she could have possibly allowed her agoraphobia to become a convenient excuse to justify her career choices and a lifestyle some would consider eccentric.

She wanted to study the thought, even if she wasn't sure she liked what the notion said about her. But before she could dissect the idea, the volume from the television in the bedroom ratcheted up a few decibels.

"Jenny." Devon's voice called over top of the sound, his tone uncharacteristically stern. Tense. "Look at this."

Already in motion, she shoved aside her personal

worries to check out the news segment Devon watched with rapt attention. Crossing the bedroom to stand beside him, she tuned into the female newscaster's words the same moment an image of Quintessence Hotel and Casino flashed onto the screen.

"The woman was found here in a private room by a maid on her morning cleaning route." The televised image changed to a stretcher being carried from the hotel and loaded into an ambulance as EMTs and hotel personnel guided the conveyance through a small crowd of cops, reporters and hotel guests.

"Police have declined to release further information about the victim's identity but have confirmed she was badly beaten. While the woman remains in critical condition, authorities are looking for a man with dark hair and medium build reported to have been near the victim's room late last night. In other news…"

As the screen changed to a local politician's speech, Devon switched the remote button off, accentuating the stunned silence in the room.

"Oh, my God." Jenny's eyes burned with the picture of the stretcher being loaded into the ambulance, knowing in her gut that the beating victim had to be one of the women she'd seen last night from Devon's hotel suite. The same woman the redhead had raised her hand to strike just before Devon and Jenny had been shut out of the encounter. "We might be the only people to have had a glimpse inside that room before—"

She couldn't even think about what must have happened last night after the threesome drew the blinds on their twisted games. And she definitely couldn't think about the fact that she'd convinced Devon they should mind their own business after they saw the first hints of what must have led to a brutal beating.

"And we might be the only people who know there were three people in the room." Devon moved toward her nightstand and picked up the phone. "Get dressed and I'll call the police."

11

"I DON'T UNDERSTAND why you won't let me take you back to your place." Devon followed Jenny into her hotel room at Quintessence late that afternoon after their trip to the police station. The local authorities hadn't been overly impressed with the information Jenny and he had to share until Devon had mapped out the exact location of the hotel window they'd been watching the night before.

By the grim expressions of everyone in the room, Devon knew his map coincided with the room where the victim had been discovered. Although still alive, the woman was heavily sedated and unavailable for questioning, making outside testimony all the more important. Since the victim hadn't been a redhead with a butterfly tattoo, police had added the information to the case file and planned to expand their search to look for that woman as well.

"I've spent enough of my life cooped up in my apartment. I volunteered to participate in a research forum on agoraphobia this week and I'm not quitting the group until we're done." Jenny flung herself onto a bar stool at the kitchen counter, her long brown skirt swirling with the abrupt movement as she jammed the heels of knee-high boots around the shiny metal footrest. "Besides, the seminars are helping me."

"If ever there was a time to be scared, a time that warranted staying at home, this is it." He couldn't understand her adamancy. He'd lined up one rational argument after another on the ride back to the hotel and she'd shot them all down. "Even if our identities remain anonymous to the public, the news of informants working with the police will reach the media soon. That's bound to make the perpetrator nervous."

"But there's a good chance the assailant already left the hotel." Jenny flipped open the room service menu and studied the offerings. "And even if she didn't, *and* she finds out that there were witnesses, she'll have no way of knowing who we are."

"Maybe. Except that smart criminals always have an eye out for their own best interests to cover their butts." He tugged the room service menu out her hands just enough to make her look up at him. To recognize how serious fingering a bad guy could be. "Whoever did this was confident enough about not getting caught to commit a crime on an upscale resort property with security cameras on every entrance twenty-four hours a day. That means whoever did this doesn't look like riffraff and doesn't have a record since even now the police will be scouring the videotape and the guest registry for possible suspects and anyone with a violent history."

"And you don't understand why I can't cut and run back home even though I've spent my whole life there, right?" She relinquished the menu to him, folding her hands into a knot on the counter as she held his gaze.

He let his silence speak for him because he couldn't see her point when her safety was at stake. What happened to the damn phobia she was supposed to suffer from?

"I'm tired of taking the path of least resistance just because it's easier. That's why I wanted to go to the Tower of Fear last night, and why I have to finish the conference."

"Why now? Why this week? Can't you sign on for some other conference or seminar?"

"No." She shook her head, her lips flattening into a straight line. "Even if I wasn't participating in the research seminar this week, I wouldn't go. Some key part of my phobia started to crumble Monday night when you showed up in my room and now that there's a chink in the barrier of my fears, I'm not going to settle for tapping away with a chisel in the hopes I hack off another piece. I'm getting out the sledgehammer and I won't stop swinging until I've cleared a permanent path through it."

"Even if it makes you the target of some kind of sadistic twosome still on the prowl?" Devon could watch out for her while they were here, but she'd be safer all the way around in Seaside Heights with her vigilant neighbor to keep an eye on her.

"That could have happened whether I came back to the hotel or not." Her fingers trembled slightly as she pulled her jacket off and slung it on the chair beside her, making him feel like crap for raking her over the coals about this. "But we did the right thing in going to the police. We just have to hope we gave them enough to catch this creepy pair."

"They will." He wanted to reassure her, to take away that tremor in her fingers, but how could he know what kind of a job local police would do? Like with any career, there must be cops who were highly skilled professionals and others who'd just barely slid through the screening process.

What if this case had been assigned to the police officer equivalent of a Dave Brady—a guy who was more flash than substance when it came to the job? The thought made his gut roil.

His phone rang before he could chase away the shadows in her eyes and he wished he hadn't spent so much time trying to talk her out of staying at the hotel when what she needed was reassurance. But then, he'd always sucked at understanding women.

Just ask his ex-wife.

"Baines." He answered on the second ring, slower than normal thanks to a hell of a lot more on his mind than engineering.

"Yeah, Hal here." The senior engineer who served on the board launched right into his concerns. "I don't know if we're going to be able to pull that second vote together anytime soon with the board. Roy Scott called this morning and said his wife wants to go out of town next week and almost everybody else has the conference for the rest of this week. I think you're fighting an uphill battle on this one."

Shit. As much as he didn't need these problems now, Devon couldn't walk away from his company yet.

"So let him phone in his vote after I have the chance to talk to him. Is he in the office today so I can meet with him?" Maybe he could talk Jenny into going with him under the guise of desensitizing herself to more places. The Shore Engineers offices were an hour south of here, but maybe he could even persuade her to come with him.

"He's scouting a new job site this week before Dave takes over the project management. Some plastic manufacturer." On the other end of the phone, Hal exchanged a few words with another person before coming back on the line. "Sorry about that, Dev, but if I can do anything else to help out, let me know."

The line disconnected before Devon could tell him that wasn't good enough.

"Everything okay?" Jenny's voice pulled him out of his dark mood, reminding him his first priority needed to be protecting her from whatever scumbag sadists prowled the hotel.

But maybe there was a chance he could still muscle his way back on top at Shore Engineers and keep an eye on her at the same time.

"Fine. But I've got to run down a guy I work with tonight if I want any shot at keeping Brady from sending my company into the toilet."

Why did his professional life have to yank him around by the balls when he met someone like Jenny? He'd far rather keep an eye on her with so much upheaval in the hotel. Plus he'd like to see what surprises tonight held in store for a couple of insomniacs, but the situation with his company couldn't wait. He needed to see the seniormost board member of Shore Engineers.

"Do you have to leave?" Striking a match, she lit one of her scented candles.

"I know you'll want to check out the workshops on tap for tomorrow, but as long as the conference day is over for right now, I wondered if you would consider coming for a ride with me?"

Damn but he hoped he could talk her into it, because leaving her alone at the hotel felt more and more risky with some vague, unnamed danger creeping closer.

THE EASIER CHOICE would have been to go with Devon tonight.

Jenny flipped through her conference handouts later that evening and half regretted her decision to stay at the hotel while he met up with a colleague in Wildwood. She felt more physically safe with him than she had at any time in her life, so the thought of exploring new terrain at his side held endless appeal. At the same time, she'd never felt so emotionally vulnerable, and that shook her to her toenails.

How could she allow herself to get deeper into a relationship that would be over after the weekend? She refused to take the easy way out anymore, preferring to confront her demons with fists raised from now on.

Seated on her living room sofa with her workshop notes in her lap, she jumped when someone knocked on her door.

Devon?

"Coming." She was halfway to the door when she remembered to think with her brain instead of her heart. "Who is it?"

"Jenny, it's Dave. Do you have a minute?"

A strange sensation unlike her usual anxiety lifted the hair at the back of her neck. Halting in the middle of the floor, she wished she hadn't announced her presence so she could have faked like no one was in the room.

It creeped her out to think he might have been watching her and Devon together while they were in the racquetball court last night. She wasn't letting Dave in, but she picked up her key ring and the small, extendable stick that could turn into a weapon with the flick of a switch.

"No." She approached slowly now, measuring her words to the man she'd exchanged multiple e-mails with, the man she'd once imagined would be her lover. "It's been a long day for me so I'm going to turn in early."

"Yeah?" His warm laughter carried through the door. "What's early for you...2:00 a.m.? Three?"

Of course he knew she never slept at night. She'd composed most of her notes to him in the hours before sunrise. She thumbed the switch on her small stick weapon, thinking she probably didn't need it after all, but holding it made her feel more secure. In control.

"The conference caught up to me, I guess." She refused to feel guilty about lying to a man who'd dumped her on the first date. Let him think whatever he wished about why she wouldn't open the door.

"Okay. I'd like to apologize in person for what happened the other night, but I don't blame you for not wanting to see me."

A rustling noise sounded through the door, making her curious.

"I'm leaving some flowers out here for you and I'm genuinely sorry for excusing myself the other night when we met for drinks. The waitress was actually an old girlfriend of mine and she came on to me when you left to use the bathroom."

Jenny waited, not ready to forgive him by any stretch, but she did remember how the waitress had flirted with him that night.

"Are you still there?" Clearing his throat, he forged ahead. "She even threatened to make you uncomfortable if I didn't see her again, so by the time you came back she'd kind of ruined the evening for me. I know she's pretty bitter and I didn't want her to upset you when I knew it took a lot of courage for you to come to your conference."

Frowning, Jenny half wished she could see his face to weigh his expression in the performance but she didn't want him to hear her leaning on the door to look out the peephole. No sense letting him think she was interested, especially since she wasn't buying the act.

She'd thought all along something had been going on between him and the waitress, so what if there was a shred of truth to the tale?

"You gave me the wrong e-mail address," she reminded him, knowing there were a million better ways to handle the situation the way he chose.

Even if his ploy *had* led her to Devon.

"I didn't think you'd e-mail me so soon after the date and once Devon Baines leaves the company, the D B at Shore Engineers address will revert to me." His voice drifted through the doorway, soft but audible as if he leaned against the wood mere inches from where she stood. "Besides, my father and his sick sense of humor gave me my current company address with an ID of Hercules since the old man never found much to admire in his only son. I ask you, if your screen name was Hercules, would you spread it around?"

She caught herself smiling and stopped. She refused to be charmed by him when Devon disliked the guy with vehemence. Besides, in all her online conversations with David, he'd never said anything as sweet or as insightful about his formative years as Devon had shared with her under the boardwalk the night before.

Still, Dave's explanation about the address made sense.

"I don't know, Dave." She would be honest with him even though he hadn't shown her the same courtesy earlier that week. "I would have appreciated it if you'd just been straight with me."

"I was nervous about meeting you and I made a bad call. I admit it." He gave the door a light tap with his hand and then his voice sounded farther away. "But my former girlfriend was apparently fired today anyway, so you don't need to worry about her giving you any trouble. Take care, Jenny. Sorry for everything."

His footsteps sounded in the corridor as he walked away, leaving her with a mixture of relief and confusion. The justifications he'd offered for his behavior seemed reasonable. Why would he have even bothered to apologize to her if he'd given her the wrong e-mail address on purpose?

Still, his apology didn't extend to skulking in the hallway outside the racquetball court last night. Had his presence there been coincidence? Or did he have some reason for sticking close to her this week? Maybe he'd simply been waiting for a window of opportunity to make amends after their disastrous first date.

Opening the door to her suite, she peered out into the hall to find a vase of white tulips and miniature pink tea roses. Very pretty. She lifted the container to inhale the fragrance and brought the flowers into her room, deciding she would give Dave Brady the benefit of the doubt even if she had no intention of ever dating him.

Now that she'd met him in person she couldn't deny a certain strange vibe from him, an inexplicable unease that could be rooted in her wealth of personal paranoias, Devon's strong dislike of him or basic individual chemistry that governed who she was attracted to. Her instincts might be more overactive than the average person's, but she usually had accurate character judgment and that particular voice in her head cautioned her where Dave was concerned.

Walking the vase of flowers into her bedroom, Jenny settled them on the dresser and told herself that same annoying voice in her head was the one that told her she could trust Devon with her person but not so much with her heart. It was a damned annoying voice she'd rather muzzle, but that inbred sense of caution would keep her from making the mistakes that had broken her mother's heart. No man would dazzle Jenny with sex and romance only to peer down his arrogant nose at her perceived weaknesses.

Jenny had worked too hard to establish a strong sense of self despite the clinical labels put on her by the dozens of doctors her mother had dragged her to see as a child. Who knew how many of her supposed illnesses had been real and how many had been well faked by her mother before Jenny grew old enough to articulate her lack of symptoms to medical professionals when her mother left the room? Of course, that turning point only made her mother more inventive, encouraging her to take her daughter to psychologists instead. Jenny had been diagnosed at various times with obsessive-compulsive disorder, an antisocial complex—with good reason, she'd always thought—and eventually an Electra complex that completely grossed her out and put an end to her patience with her mother marching her around to every shrink in town.

No question, Jenny's peace of mind had been hard won when all the world seemed to conspire to assure her she was crazy. Except for the Serivolos next door, who'd always believed Jenny's sanity and had rewarded her survival of another doctor appointment with chocolate chip cookies and a few commiserating *tsks* on her behalf.

Pacing back out to the kitchen in her suite, Jenny eyed the multitude of medicine bottles near the sink with new eyes. She ran her finger along the labels from an alternative healing center. They were natural supplements that she'd once convinced herself were to boost her good health. But did she really need the extra vitamins? The St. John's wort? Or was she still letting old fears rule her choices?

With slow deliberation, she picked up the waste-basket to the height of the counter top and swept all the bottles off the granite into the trash. This was the week she would banish each and every old fear and birth the independent woman she was born to be. No more being ruled by the past.

And if that meant taking a gamble with her heart, too, maybe she owed it to herself to at least explore the option. God knows Devon hadn't taken a step back from their relationship since that first morning-after, which he'd explained. And apologized to her.

Maybe she shouldn't be so quick to diagnose every relationship as a possible disaster. An independent woman didn't medicate herself against real life or she just might miss out on an opportunity for real love.

DEVON NEEDED to get out of Roy Scott's house.

Roy's opinion remained crucial to Devon's campaign to stay with the company, but ever since Devon had shown up on his doorstep to plead a case in private, the guy's wife had been coming on to him whenever Roy wasn't looking.

Now, Devon listened to the manager in charge of structural engineering as he droned on about the im-portance of corporate integrity and commitment to the Shore Engineers mission. All of which had no bearing on why Dave Brady ought to be leading a company purely on the basis of his genes. And— according to Hal—a flair for closing a deal.

Devon drained his martini and pried Melinda Scott's fingers off his thigh under the dining room table. Was she out of her mind? Maybe she assumed he was fair game since he was leaving the company, but she'd proven amazingly undeterred by his brush-offs. And while he wasn't attracted to her, he also couldn't help the automatic reaction to a hand grazing his fly.

Which only served to piss him off.

Grinding his teeth, he interrupted Roy's endless monologue to stress what he hoped to gain by driving all the way out here tonight. Alone.

"Roy, all I'm asking is for you to reconsider giving Brady the keys to the kingdom." Devon spared a dark look at manhunting Melinda fluffing her short, dark curls while Roy stirred his olives around his glass and turned his lower lip out in thought. "I can e-mail you a five-year growth plan under my direction if you'd like to see more development in that area, but I can't walk away from the company John worked so hard to build just because it would be easier to set up shop on my own."

Shoving back from the table, he batted the petite brunette's fingers away as she raked her nails over his belt, drawing Roy's attention with her high, musical laugh.

"Is she bothering you, Baines?" The older man's eyes lit with ill-disguised fire, his affection—or lust?—for his younger wife obvious. "Damn it, woman, we're talking work. Can't you amuse yourself somewhere else until we're finished?"

"I'm feeling very amused right here." She winked at her husband and leaned across the table to pat his hand, pressing ample cleavage against the wood in an obvious display showcased by a satin dressing gown and filmy little robe that covered exactly nothing.

Devon didn't mind PDAs exactly, but the vibe between this couple creeped him out and he found himself really wishing he hadn't sought Roy outside the office.

"I'll e-mail you those things we discussed tonight." Devon backed up a step, thinking the drive back to Atlantic City sounded a hell of a lot more fun than sitting here. Even if he'd be working on a stupid five-year plan tonight instead of getting naked with Jenny. "I'm going to take off now."

He should have just made a run for it instead of announcing an intention to leave since the words seemed to call Melinda from the long, hot looks she gave Roy. Glancing up, she rose to her feet.

"I'll see you out."

"That's okay. I've got it." He scooped a handful of papers off the end of the table where he'd first launched his appeal to Roy tonight.

"I insist." She helped him retrieve the papers, her

lush curves brushing against him as she worked. And, with his files held hostage in her neatly manicured fingertips, he didn't see a polite escape from Melinda's escort.

Tension clenching his muscles, he pivoted on his heel to make tracks toward the door, his colleague's wife sticking close enough to him to breathe suggestive—explicit—whispers against his back.

Plowing through the front door, Devon closed the distance to his truck with long strides, snatching the papers out of Melinda's hand the moment she arrived at the vehicle.

To hell with being polite. She'd sure made no effort.

"Look, I'm not comfortable with the sexual antics." Tossing the papers into the passenger seat, Devon wanted to make sure there were no misunderstandings. "I respect your husband and I'm one of those guys who thinks marriage is a big deal so I'd never go near another man's wife in a million years even if that man seemed okay with it."

Even if he *had* been attracted. Which he wasn't. But there was no point in making this a personal issue when—on ethics alone—he'd never break that social contract.

Social contract? Hell, he was no Bible thumper, but even he recalled this one was a commandment. Carved in stone, for crying out loud.

"But it just so happens you're near me right now anyway, aren't you?" Smiling wolfishly, she stood outside in the paved driveway wearing nothing more than a long satin dressing gown with a flimsy matching robe thrown over top.

The slit in the side of both garments went high up her thigh, however, showcasing her leg when she walked or stood in a siren's pose with one knee bent the way she did now. Her fingers smoothed over her hip down to that high slit in the fabric and peeled aside the material. She flashed him a view of sheer red panties that exposed…

Well damn.

He would have walked away because he wasn't tempted by this aggressive woman who belonged to a friend. Except that, right beside her shaved mound visible beneath the transparent panties, Melinda Scott had a butterfly tattoo.

12

"YOU *SAW* HER TATTOO?"

Jenny had to hack the words out over gasping breaths since she nearly spewed her ginger ale when he sprung the news on her the next day. And after she'd managed to swallow her drink, she'd gagged anew at the thought of Devon seeing the bright yellow and orange butterfly perched to the side of another woman's cha-cha.

He'd cornered her in between the afternoon sessions to talk to her, but she'd never suspected he'd come out with something like this in a vacant meeting room near the hotel business offices.

"It wasn't like that." Devon reached to pat her back, but Jenny ducked his hand and steadied herself on one of the vacant chairs sitting around a large boardroom table, preferring to cough her way through a conversation she didn't want to have.

"Sorry, but I can't imagine any innocent way a woman's most intimate places are revealed during casual conversation."

"I told you, she was coming on to me all night.

Another reason I wish you had joined me on the trip to Roy's house so maybe she would have stayed away. The woman is a menace."

"Pardon me if I don't feel sorry for you." Getting herself under control as she took a more leisurely sip of her ginger ale, Jenny told herself she hadn't gotten that close to Devon, so what did it matter if he had messed around with another woman.

Except she had gotten close to Devon, had even contemplated seeing where the relationship led after their week at Quintessence Hotel was finished. And damn it, this hurt.

"She followed me out to my truck when I tried to leave and when I told her I had no interest in a married woman under any circumstances, she—"

"Yes?" Jenny couldn't even begin to picture what came next, her heart clenching as she waited for details of his betrayal.

"She kind of swept aside a nightgown thing she wore and flashed me her goods as if that would bring me in line." To his credit, he looked more than a little disgusted.

Even Jenny had to admit this woman's—Melinda Scott's—techniques sounded a little over the top. Sure, men were visual creatures, but Jenny liked to think that at least a few of them preferred some mystery in the chase. If a woman simply revealed everything all at once, what did she have left in her personal arsenal to use in tantalizing a man?

"She lifted her nightgown in the middle of a driveway while her husband waited inside the house?" Were there women who would be so bold? So uncaring about a spouse and the marriage they shared?

"Call me crazy, but I think her husband knows what she's like and doesn't mind."

"How could a man not mind when his wife is offering herself to other guys? In front of his house, for God's sake?"

Devon tipped the door to the meeting room shut, closing out the sudden barrage of people in the hall. He pulled a high-backed chair out from under the long table to offer her a seat but she was too keyed up to stay still.

"I've asked myself the same thing because the woman has hit on me before but always much more subtly. Last night she was very overt—right in front of him, even—and I think he must like that she's kinky." Devon speared a hand through his dark hair, clearly wound up.

Exasperated.

Only now did she notice the shadows beneath his eyes that hinted at his long night. Because of worry? Or because the kinky woman had her way with him into the wee hours of morning?

But even as the green-eyed monster inside her formed the question, her rational side quickly dismissed it. He'd been even more upset about the threesome incident two nights ago than she had been. He would have never touched a woman who might have participated—or stood by and watched—while another person was being brutalized.

"You don't think her husband could have been the man in the black boxers that we saw through the window, do you?"

"The police asked me that, too."

"You went to the police?" Jenny decided she needed that seat after all. Her week of personal growth and self-indulgent sex was rapidly turning scary.

"Of course." Devon leaned back to sit against the edge of the table, his trousers stretched taut over strong thighs. "The butterfly looked exactly the same to me. I had no choice but to report what I saw, even if Melinda Scott isn't a redhead."

"Might have been a wig," Jenny mused, wishing she could have spent all week long in bed with Devon so they'd never seen the strange threesome through the window. As much as she'd like to retreat there now to test the strength of those muscular thighs for herself, she knew they needed to talk. Maybe she could help rule out Melinda or confirm her as a possible suspect if she knew more. "And her kinky leanings fit the profile. You think this woman could go both ways?"

"Damned if I know." He smoothed a hand down his silver and black tie stitched with a subtle pattern of wrenches. "I've never seen her come on to another woman and I've never seen her in a wig, but I usually avoid her like the plague ever since she groped me in front of my ex-wife."

Jenny blinked.

Thought before she spoke.

And then decided that there was no way she could ignore that huge piece of information he'd chunked out into their conversation like it was no big deal.

"You've been married?"

"That hasn't come up before, has it?" Devon shook his head. "Wait, don't answer that, I know it hasn't come up yet because I've been distracted this week thinking about the mess I'm leaving behind at my company and I haven't made enough effort to get to know you—or let you know me."

Jenny thought about their unorthodox way of getting to know one another. They'd been too busy tearing off one another's clothes to appreciate the people inside. A first for her. And while it had been fun, perhaps she should have made more of an effort to talk to Devon.

"How long were you married?" Jenny wondered what kind of woman he'd chosen. "No, wait. First tell me how long you've been divorced."

The gaping hole in her knowledge of him demonstrated her own oversights as much as his. While she wished he would have thought to mention it sooner, why hadn't she ever thought to ask about his past dating experiences?

Sure she was a novice when it came to relationships, but she had enough common sense to know she should be talking to him about those things instead of simply shutting down her brain whenever they were together in favor of pure sensation.

Once again, she'd been hiding behind her fears, playing games of avoidance. When would she ever learn?

"The divorce is just over a year old. The marriage lasted four years even though we probably both knew it wasn't working after the first anniversary." Devon's hands gripped the edge of the table, his forearms flexing with his hold. "You may have noticed I'm not much of a people person. I put in a lot of hours at work even when things are going well for me, but when I run into personal trouble, I don't even come up for air at the office. So Lori and I sort of coasted on fumes for a few years before she left."

"She left you?" Jenny could understand the allure of work when a person's private life sucked. But as much as she empathized with Devon, she suspected that together her and Devon would both be too quick to run for cover at the first sign of problems and *someone* had to be willing to fight for a relationship.

Especially if that relationship was a marriage.

"Yes. She got tired of my…" He hesitated, his jaw muscle working overtime before he spoke again, "Physical needs."

"Sex drive?"

"I could ignore a lot of problems, but I couldn't

ignore the total lack of sex." He huffed out a long breath. "Not that I'm Joe Testosterone or anything, but our visions of the role sex should play in our relationship became so disparate that she withdrew altogether even though when we first met I would at least be welcomed into her bed on the nights before her spa days so she could…I don't know…fix herself afterward."

"What do you mean, 'fix herself'?" Jenny didn't follow. Although she suspected that many women's and men's sex drives didn't permanently match up. Wasn't that an irrefutable part of biology? A chemical and hormonal legacy governed by genes?

"She thought sex messed her up. Made her feel less pretty or something since I usually smudged a just-painted toenail or breathed too heavily on a facial treatment mask. She never considered sex fun and eventually it turned into the defining feature of our relationship, the line that could not be crossed." Devon shrugged. "We probably would have parted a lot more amiably if she hadn't waited until we both grew resentful. She ended up marrying her esthetician."

"You deserved better than that." Reaching for his hand, she covered his fingers with her own, rolling her high-backed chair closer to where he leaned against the table.

"So did she. We made a mistake. Sometimes the things that look good on paper don't necessarily add up in real life."

Silence fell between them. Jenny understood him well enough to know how much a flawed equation would frustrate him. His wife's defection must have stung, but his own inability to solve the problems would have eaten away at him long afterward.

"Now that I think about it," Devon continued, "Maybe I'd been searching so hard for the perfect home life after the way I grew up that I couldn't appreciate the big picture of what marriage gave me."

"I'm sorry," Jenny offered finally, remembering she'd veered off course in their conversation to follow the thread of his ex-wife. "About the divorce and about jumping to the wrong conclusion that you were trying to hide it from me. I know this relationship has gotten off to a wild start."

"You don't hear me complaining." He turned his hand over beneath hers. Lining up their palms and then their fingers. "Maybe relationships don't have to add up. Maybe it's better if you can be with someone without having to think so damn hard all the time."

She stared at their matched palms, her fingers falling short of his, his knuckles bowing out wider than hers. And yet the fit made her heart pound harder, her skin warm with the idea of lining up the rest of their bodies so carefully.

"In that case we must be on to something good." She rose from her chair, needing to get closer to him. "Because I can't remember doing much thinking when you're around since I'm too busy feeling things."

"Is that so?" He drew her between his splayed thighs, one hand dipping low on her hips as he guided her where he wanted her. "I've been thinking enough things for both of us then. Because right now I'm thinking about how good you're going to taste." He leaned close to nip her lower lip. "And the whole way home last night I kept thinking about how much I wanted to knock on your door and wake you up to be with you."

It would have been so easy to lose herself in his words, his warm scent. To not think.

But the fact remained that Devon hadn't brought her into the vacant meeting space to seduce her or even to share the story of his divorce. Last night he'd gone to the police for the second time in two days and that scared her. The danger lurking in Quintessence Hotel and Casino could easily be connected to Devon or his company.

"I wouldn't have minded the wake-up call." She hadn't slept well anyway. "But you never told me what the police said about the woman with the tattoo. Were they going to check her out? Question her?"

"They said that kind of tattoo is too common to bother everybody who might have one, but they did say they'd review the hotel's security tapes and look specifically for Melinda. If they find she was in the hotel that night—either as a brunette or a redhead—they'll definitely want to talk to her."

Satisfied, Jenny trailed her fingers down his

thighs on either side of her, savoring the feel of rough twill against her skin and the warm male heat that came with it.

She might have leaned in for a kiss—to quit thinking—except that a cell phone rang in the hallway. She didn't even process that particular sound or tone, but apparently Devon did since he dropped his hands and set her aside.

Without a word, he sprinted out the door and into the crowded corridor.

OUTSIDE THE empty meeting room, Devon's path was cut short by a mob of at least thirty conference-goers dressed in matching shirts that read Hooked on Hypnosis as they lined up for a group photo.

He dodged around one side of the gathering, no longer hearing the ringing phone in the din of the picture-taking group. Damn.

With the memory of Jenny's almost-kiss still clinging to him, he scoured the hall for signs of Dave Brady. The bastard was following Jenny. Or him. Devon wasn't certain who, but he knew he'd never uncover the answers until he pried himself out of Jenny's arms long enough to confront the thorn in his side for more years than he cared to count.

Disgusted with himself for letting life roll over him like a freight train the past few months instead of fighting for his old mentor's company, Devon tried his trick of ringing Brady's cell but the phone rang until voice mail picked up and Devon didn't hear the echoing ring in the hall.

Which meant either his hunch was dead wrong or else Brady was on to him.

Flashbulbs popping all around, Devon made his way back toward the room where Jenny waited, frustration pounding through him with each step. He couldn't allow her to get wrapped up any deeper in his problems. She'd been so excited about her progress this week with her phobia. What if she got spooked by Brady and lost all that forward momentum?

Not that Devon cared so much about her being an adventurous spirit anymore. Her late night thrill seeking was more than enough to make him happy for as long as she trusted him to be by her side. She'd never have to leave her apartment during the day for all he cared. But she'd been so intent on her desensitization and making personal headway that he couldn't allow Brady to mess it up.

She needed to go home, far away from Quintessence Hotel and all the problems at Shore Engineers. Only then would she be safe from whatever games Brady was playing. Not to mention the twisted creep from across the courtyard two nights ago who might be involved with Melinda Scott.

Devon swallowed an involuntary shudder at the thought of some freak getting near Jenny—male or female. No more delaying to keep her by his side a little longer. He'd see her back to Seaside Heights tonight.

Pushing open the door to the meeting room he found her tapping a pen impatiently at the long table. When she heard him enter she rose to her feet, scooping up her purse and a notebook. Her belted sweater dress hugged her curves, outlining a silhouette that had left him drooling since that first night he'd seen her in garters and stockings.

"Did you see anyone?" She adjusted the purse strap on her shoulder, her eyes still on the door. "Do you think Dave is still following you?"

"He's following one of us." There was no time like the present to start making it clear to her that danger lurked here. "But I didn't catch sight of him this time. Can I walk you upstairs?"

"I was going to get together with some other women from an agoraphobia support group at the bar for drinks in a few minutes. We're going to try to stay for a whole hour." She checked her watch. "But I can meet up with you afterward."

At the hotel bar she'd be visible to Dave if he was following her. And Devon wouldn't be there to keep him away.

"I'm concerned about your safety here."

"Because of David?"

"I don't like it that he's lurking around every corner lately."

"I think he's done lurking, actually. He came to see me last night."

Devon's jaw tightened. "You spoke with him?"

Jealousy gnawed him hard as he recalled she hadn't wanted to go anywhere with *him* last night. She'd been with David instead.

"He stopped by my room."

He must have let his surprise show because she hurried to explain.

"I didn't let him in or anything, but he left flowers at my door to apologize for getting off to a rocky start that first night." She shrugged, making light of the visit that seemed like a big freaking deal to Devon. "I think that's why he may have been lurking earlier this week. He was just trying to find a window of time to make his apologies."

She bought that? Devon told himself it could be true, that the guy did have some redeeming qualities after all. But he'd known Brady a lot longer than she had and he found the story damn difficult to swallow.

"So why was his phone ringing in the hall just now?" He heard the frustration in his voice but remained powerless to disguise it.

"You said yourself that ring is the standard setting for your company phones and this hotel is crawling with engineers. Don't you think it's a strong possibility that was someone else's phone?"

No. He knew it wasn't. But how could he tell her as much without looking like a jealous jerk?

Changing strategies, he figured he'd get back to Brady later.

"What about the other danger in the hotel, Jen?"

They'd discussed this before, but the need for her to leave seemed all the more pressing now that he'd found out the woman with the butterfly tattoo was associated with Shore Engineers. What if the man who'd been in that room two nights ago was connected, too? "We gave statements to the police. Don't you think whoever assaulted that woman would be eager to silence anyone who could point the finger at him? Or her?"

He half regretted his more forceful approach on the issue when a hint of fear skittered through her hazel gaze.

"Those records are confidential." She folded her arms around herself in a protective stance.

"That doesn't mean information doesn't leak, especially if the assailant has connections." He reached for her shoulders, fingers skimming fuzzy sweater and warm woman. "Damn it, Jen, I'm not trying to scare you. I'm just trying to make you see why it makes me nervous to have you staying here. You've gotten so much out of the conference already. Why don't you let me drive you home tonight?"

Her arms unfolded again, her spine straightening.

"I can't do that."

"There's a maniac on the loose. You know, some fears were instilled in human beings for a damn good reason and this is one of them."

"I know you don't put much stock in self-help and phobias, but they are real and they suck. I'm not walking away from the most progress I've ever made with this problem because I'm scared."

"I put plenty of stock in self-help." The words stuck a little on the way out his mouth and Devon wondered if maybe he hadn't been as supportive of her efforts as he could have been. "And I think it's great that you're making changes, but don't sacrifice your safety because of some epic battle with fear. Don't you see? It's a *good* thing to be scared at times like this."

She said nothing, her eyes widening at his voice that had somehow increased in volume without his permission. Ah crap.

"Look. I know you want to beat this thing and I'd help you if you let me. I know a little about taking a company public and I could help you out with De-Luxe if you want." He knew half the reason she wanted to go through with the whole conference was to garner enough comfort with going out of her house so she could take her business to the next level. "I contributed to the paperwork making Shore a publicly traded company two years ago, even if the majority of the shares belong to the people who work there. I could share what I know to ease the process."

She took a small step back from him, but from the tension radiating off her ramrod straight posture he suspected a yawning gap had just opened wide between them.

"My business has broken industry records for

volume sold in the first five years. De-Luxe is the *one* area of my life where I definitely don't need help."

O-kay.

He'd obviously hit a hot button there, but he wasn't sure how to gain back lost ground. He still thought she should steer clear of the hotel and maybe tap her neighbor to help keep an eye out for strangers around the building.

"I just want you to consider your safety."

"By sending me home early," she clarified, tipping her head to one side to study him. "Are you sure this is about my safety and not your need for independence?"

"Hell no." How could she think that? Hadn't he told her he wanted to spend more time with her? To keep her in his life after their week together was up? "You're the one who said we needed to limit this thing between us to a week, remember? I wanted to try building something and you shut me down."

"Because you've got issues with my phobia." Hands on hips, she glared right back at him. "*Big* issues."

"But I'm not willing to just throw my hands in the air and give up because of that. I'm the man who's all about the thrill of the ride. Why can't we just see where it leads?"

Hadn't he told her those things? He knew expressing himself wasn't his strong suit, but he could have sworn he'd told her…what? That he cared about her? That he wanted more than just the thrill of great sex?

He was only just beginning to process that maybe

he hadn't told her all of the things he'd been thinking about when he realized she was headed for the door. The swish of her hips taunted him with his mistakes as she walked away.

"I'm trying my best to take bigger risks, Devon. But the one you're asking me to take is a whole lot scarier to me than staying in a strange hotel with a couple of perverts on the loose." She opened the door to a hallway grown more subdued now that conference goers had scattered for dinners or other evening plans. "That kind of risk is something I have to work up to, and no matter how much I tell myself I could be okay after the fallout, I know in my heart I'm just not there yet."

13

HALF-HIDDEN BEHIND the door to a meeting room next door, David watched Jenny walk away from loverboy Devon. Finally. The pair had been in their own meeting room for so long David had begun to wonder if they were having another kinky semipublic interlude like the one he'd witnessed on the Steel Pier three nights ago.

But the stiff set of Jenny's shoulders didn't give the impression of a woman well satisfied as she headed for the stairwell and then backtracked toward the elevator. Had Devon failed to deliver this time? Or had Jenny finally wised up and given him the boot?

David followed her from a safe distance, keeping plenty of hotel guests between them to ensure his presence remained undetected. Melinda had given him an earful about cutting his conference short before someone put the two of them together, but he had no intention of leaving Quintessence without a taste of Jenny Moore.

Once he saw her enter an elevator car going up, he hit the stairs and hoped he'd be able to catch her on the tenth floor later tonight. He'd been an idiot to let her get away earlier this week in favor of the little waitress who couldn't keep her hands off him, but he'd been fired up that night after a long dry spell without Melinda who seemed to love sex with her slavishly grateful husband as much as she liked sex with David. That night in the bar with Jenny he'd been so wound up he'd taken the outlet that seemed fastest without any regard to quality.

Then he remembered that impatience was one of many personality defects his father had pointed out to him. David had never been able to work hard enough for life's big payoffs, preferring whatever was quick and easy according to John Brady, and then griping about it later.

Screw you, old man.

Jenny was a top-notch woman. The kind of woman he should have in his life on a more permanent basis to keep him on the straight and narrow. She handled herself with grace and poise despite her phobias. Hell, maybe she could show him how to keep his demons locked in the closet on the days he wanted to be good. And on the days he wanted to be bad, well, surely he'd find a naughty streak in Ms. Moore if he applied himself to the task. Exercised a little frigging patience. He'd certainly seen tantalizing hints of her wanton side this week as he'd followed her every move with Devon Baines. Dave could afford to wait for her now that he'd eased his hunger with Sasha and then Melinda and Melinda's lady lover, too.

Swallowing down his memory of how quickly that night with Melinda and the other woman had gotten out of hand, Dave knew he needed to align himself with a more stable female as soon as possible. He needed Jenny's steadiness in his life to keep him level.

Good thing he'd made the necessary arrangements to take her far away from Atlantic City. His bags were already packed, the plane tickets purchased to a private island where he would celebrate Devon's departure from Shore Engineers and Jenny's arrival in his life.

At the top of the stairs, he made sure the hallway was clear before he entered the tenth floor where both he and Jenny had suites. Jenny should already be in her room by now and he didn't want to have a chance meeting with her until he was ready. He needed to speak with the Quintessence management about Sasha first since apparently his first complaint about her hadn't succeeded in getting the waitress fired the way he'd hoped. The last thing he needed was a jilted waitress crying to her friends about David being too rough during their night together now that the hotel had been the scene of a brutal beating two nights ago.

An attack that had little to do with him and everything to do with Melinda's perverted tastes. Damn the woman. She'd outlasted her usefulness now that she'd talked her husband into voting David in place as the company CEO.

He wouldn't pay for someone else's mistakes just when he was getting his life on track professionally. And with Jenny Moore in his bed, maybe he'd finally set things straight on a personal level, too. After he settled Jenny comfortably in the private cabin he'd found for their rendezvous, he would see about taking care of Melinda and Devon. His life would be simpler, cleaner with the two of them out of the picture.

Perhaps he could convince Melinda to coax Devon into her bed and let Hal catch them in the act. No. The old guy didn't have the heart to finish off the problem as effectively as David would like. Perhaps David would simply renew his love of shooting fish in a barrel once Devon and Melinda were in bed together.

A neat, efficient solution.

Tonight, once David had softened up Jenny and given her the satisfaction she'd been craving this week, he'd take her away from all the nasty people in Atlantic City so she wouldn't have to see her lover's dangerous side.

As HER CLOCK approached midnight, Jenny turned up the volume on her CD player and let Tchaikovsky carry her away. This was no night for Debussy and Chopin. She felt dark and dangerous as she packed her last suitcase for the drive back to Seaside Heights. She'd already stashed the big trunk in her car. Now she only had this last bag to fill while she listened to her music.

Sure she'd be charged for the room when she didn't sleep there, but leaving when the hotel was less busy suited her just fine. She'd rather feel the fury of her thwarted romantic notions than allow herself to be disappointed or—worse—depressed. No, better that she indulge her wild emotions in the impassioned strains of the Fourth Symphony than risk the heartbreak sure to coincide with a more romantic song.

Not that she had any right to be heartbroken, she reminded herself as she smoothed the creases from a length of red silk she'd brought to wrap around the hotel lampshade beside her bed. *She'd* been the one to tell Devon it wouldn't work between them even though he'd offered to give a relationship a try, so it wasn't as though he'd walked away from her.

Did that mean she was simply too much of a coward to face future rejection? Or that she was such an expert about love she could already see the inevitable end of their relationship based on a few incredible days together?

Not bloody likely.

Still, she could only get so much of her life together at once and being brave and bold enough to take a chance on a future with Devon ranked as something she couldn't tackle right now. She'd only just learned how to desensitize herself to new surroundings and she had a lot to think about with taking the business public despite Joe Serivolo's attempt to discourage her on the move. Taking a risk with Devon on top of all her other goals felt daunting and she was woman enough to admit it.

Packing up her conference brochures on top of her clothes, Jenny wasn't leaving tonight because he wanted her to go home, however. This retreat had nothing to do with danger lurking in the hotel or fears of retribution from whoever had beaten the poor woman who still lay unconscious in the hospital. Now that her forum on agoraphobia had finished its last meeting, Jenny simply hoped to avoid another confrontation with Devon because she couldn't risk him demanding to accompany her back home.

His offer to help her take De-Luxe public had hurt in unexpected ways. Sure he'd offered to be generous since he was busy enough with his own career. But part of her couldn't help but wonder if another reason he'd volunteered his aid was to make sure she beat her agoraphobia and didn't turn into a recluse like his mother. She hated fearing that kind of scenario, but it was difficult to tell where her phobia-inspired fears ended and normal insecurities began.

Jenny double-checked the empty hotel closet, deciding once she retrieved her CDs she'd be ready to leave. She'd said she wanted to get everything she could out of the conference, but after walking away from Devon tonight she'd realized that she'd learned more about herself this week than any mere psych seminar could offer. She had the tools for change in her hand already. She only needed to use them.

Stuffing the CDs in her purse, she plucked the gardenia Devon had given her out of a glass on the kitchen counter. She could take it home and tuck the wilting bloom in a drawer to make the most of the scent. Surely that was why she felt compelled to bring along the drooping flower and not because of any sappy sentimentality.

Yeah, right.

She rolled her suitcase out into the corridor and turned toward the elevator, patting the outside pocket of her luggage to make sure her key ring was there with the small baton. Once she got down to the lobby she'd have a valet bring her car around, but it didn't hurt to be careful.

The elevator chimed its arrival, but at the last second, Jenny pivoted on her heel. If ever there'd been a night to brave the stairs, this was it. Making the trip down ten flights would be the ultimate way to flip off her agoraphobia, a fitting cap to her week of desensitization and self-improvement.

Wheeling the bag behind her, Jenny reached for the door to the stairwell and hesitated as she thought she heard another door open in the hall behind her. But when she turned to look, all remained quiet. The tenth floor was probably glad to be rid of her and her loudly played classical tunes.

Shrugging off the heebie-jeebies the same way

she had in those painful moments of sitting in the lobby bar by herself, Jenny channeled those dark and wild emotions Tchaikovsky had churned up earlier to force her feet down the stairs. Her suitcase weighed too much for this exercise, but there could be no stopping a woman hell-bent on stepping out of her shadows.

One flight down she paused to rest her arm after banging her bag along too many steps. Only then did she become aware of someone else's presence in the stairwell.

A light shuffle of steps behind her. A breath, maybe.

Turning, she came face-to-face with David Brady a mere five steps behind her. She didn't know whether to be relieved or even more scared.

Her breath caught in her throat the way it sometimes did during a bout of social anxiety. For a moment, she couldn't speak. Couldn't ask him what he was doing here.

That didn't surprise her.

What *did* surprise her was that he didn't say anything to her either. Instead, he took a few slow—menacing?—steps closer until he was all but a foot away. Devon's words about fear being a natural defense mechanism reverberated through her head. He'd said sometimes she needed to pay attention to the alarm, not write it off to her phobia.

She wanted to speak, to ask David what he wanted

now, since she'd thought they settled everything after he apologized. But she was trapped in some kind of mild panic moment as he leaned closer—intimidatingly close—and planted his lips on hers in a kiss that swallowed her silent scream.

THE SHRILL SHRIEK of his cell phone made Devon lose his train of thought in cyber solitaire. Not that he'd been thinking about the cards. He'd picked a spot at the lobby bar to keep an eye out for Jenny and her friends hours ago but she'd never shown up and he'd found himself sending e-mails to colleagues at Shore for support, plotting his strategy to win back his position.

"Baines." He folded down his laptop screen out of habit.

"Dev, it's Hal." The Shore board member's voice scratched over the receiver.

"You sound like death warmed over."

"Too many cigarettes and not enough sleep. I'm getting too old for the conference scene."

"Socializing is a bitch." Which was why he sat in an overpopulated bar playing solitaire. "Give me a computer over conversation any day of the week."

Unless socializing involved Jenny. Then…that was a whole different story. He only hoped he hadn't blown it for good with her tonight by pushing her to go home.

"I just heard from Roy Scott."

Devon straightened, forcing aside thoughts of all

the mistakes he'd made with Jen this week and the din of conversation and music emanating from the bar.

"What's up?"

"There's no way we're going to be able to get the board together for a vote before your resignation takes effect, Dev. Roy's wife has just been hauled into the local police station for questioning and he's pretty broken up."

"Melinda?" Devon's gut twisted to think she'd really had something to do with the beating the other night. Roy Scott was such a stand-up guy. He didn't deserve the kind of public scrutiny this would no doubt bring his way.

"Yeah. Something about a witness putting her at the scene of the assault in the hotel the other night." Hal hacked out a dry cough. "Sounds bogus to me, but Roy seemed worried. He asked for a leave of absence for the next week or so."

Putting David Brady at the helm with no senior board member looking over his shoulder for at least a week. God knows what kind of damage he could do in that time.

Knowing his instincts were right about the guy, Devon still didn't want to see him fail if the consequences meant ruining everything his father had worked so hard to develop. He swapped his phone to his other ear in a lame attempt to drown out the squeal of a couple of women at a table nearby and the *cha-ching* of electronic darts against one wall.

"Roy was heading up that big project off-site next week. If you need me to stick around a little longer to oversee the job, let me know." Even if it meant working for a Brady for a few more days. Too damn much pride had gotten Devon into this situation in the first place since he hadn't even bothered to press the board to hire him.

He wouldn't make that mistake again.

"Thanks, Dev. I'll let Dave know you offered."

Devon disconnected and pocketed his phone, wondering if he should give Jenny a call to share the news. He knew better than to show up at her door after her cool rebuff earlier, but she'd been as unsettled by what they'd witnessed through the window that night as him. She'd want to know about Melinda's arrest and she deserved to hear any information about the case.

"Can I get you anything else, sir?" The petite brunette waitress removed his beer bottle from the table and wiped off the ring it left behind next to his laptop.

"Just the check." He pulled out his phone again, needing to speak to Jenny whether the feeling was mutual or not.

Her safety was more important than any miscommunication between them. More important than his heart that warned him he wouldn't see her again after she left the conference this weekend.

"You're friends with the tall blonde, aren't you?" the waitress asked as she scribbled on her notepad and then tore off his bill to lay on the table in front of him. "She's kind of elegant-looking with hair about to here?"

The woman made a chopping motion against her chin.

"You know her?" Devon waited to see what she had to say before he said anything about Jenny in an effort to protect her privacy.

"I've been meaning to speak to her or give her a message. Her name is Jenny, right?"

The prickle of warning along the back of his neck made him edgy. Whatever she had to say, Devon wanted to hear it.

"Yes. I'll be speaking with her soon." Especially if he had an excuse for knocking on her door. He'd be too glad to play messenger boy for the woman— Sasha according to her name tag. "Want me to tell her something?"

She balanced her serving tray on her hip and bent closer.

"Just tell her that guy she had drinks with the other night is bad news."

Devon tensed, the back of his neck tickling a warning at the serious note in Sasha's voice. She had to mean Brady since Jenny had been with Devon the rest of the week.

"What do you mean? Bad news how?"

"Just that he's a creep." She straightened as a patron from the other side of the bar waved for her attention. "I spent some time with him a few nights ago and he scared me when he sort of checked out on me mentally and started calling me 'Jenny.' I got a freaky sort of vibe that she might want to watch her step around him."

Dread washed through his gut, icy cold and uneasy. He wanted to quiz her what she meant about Dave being rough and how she knew, but she melted into the Friday bar crowd growing bigger and more raucous as midnight approached.

Packing up his laptop and a few papers he'd spread on the table, Devon jammed everything into his briefcase and dialed Jenny's room.

No answer.

Had she ventured out on her own? Or was Dave making late-night visits to her room again?

The thought made him shove his way through the crowd more forcefully, the adrenaline pumping through his veins now bearing nothing in common with the thrill ride rush he'd pursued so often. This fear was the real deal, the sick, gut-wrenching twist of his insides that made him sprint through the lobby once he cleared the barroom overflow and hit the elevator button to go upstairs.

He didn't need to analyze the facts or solve any stupid equations. Jenny had helped him get his head out of his ass—away from a job he'd always allowed to consume him—long enough to recognize his emotions, to pay attention when his instincts twitched.

Stabbing the redial button with obsessive repetition, he finally broke the chain of calls to her room to phone the front desk. She hadn't checked out yet. For the hell of it, he asked to be connected to Brady's room. He wasn't in either.

A fact which only made Devon's scalp prick with wariness all the more.

The elevator stopped on the third floor and Devon thought he'd lose his mind waiting for a family with three teenage kids to pile into the car. They held the doors to argue with one of them who refused to get in for one inane reason or another. Devon thought about taking the stairs, but the girl finally flounced inside with the others and they all piled off two floors up.

Thank God.

He hit the long corridor on the tenth floor at a run. His brain finally balanced the equation that hadn't made sense to him before. Melinda Scott was an aggressive manhunter. Her husband was the head of the Shore Engineers board.

Wouldn't Dave Brady be a natural target for her affections? And Devon didn't think for a moment that Brady would tell her no out of some sense of honor. He would have seen an ally on the board and jumped at the chance to coerce her into putting in a good word with Roy.

If the two of them were having an affair, Devon would bet his shares in Shore Engineers that the man with Melinda and the woman who'd been assaulted was the same man Sasha called a roughneck.

And oh, God, Devon would kill the bastard when he found him.

Devon skidded to a stop in front of 1016 and pounded on the door.

"Jenny." He shouted her name, not caring who heard.

No music. No lights from inside.

There was no way in hell she'd be sleeping yet.

She must have gone out. With Dave?

Devon punched in Brady's cell phone number and listened. Nothing.

Wait. Had that been a half ring he'd heard in the opposite direction from the elevator? Or were his ears ringing from stone-cold fear?

Dropping his briefcase in front of her door, he took off in that direction. With each footfall on the carpeted floor, he prayed that Jenny was okay because he'd never forgive himself if he'd missed his chance to tell her he wanted more than wild sex with her, more than the thrill of taking her clothes off under a public boardwalk.

He wanted Jenny to be safe so he could tell her how much he wanted the chance to love her.

14

Jenny Moore—Dead Woman.

She would not let that happen, even though it felt as though Dave Brady was trying to suffocate her with his kiss that threatened to crack her jaw. She'd tried biting him, but she could have sworn that only enflamed him somehow since he simply burrowed harder against her mouth, slamming her head into the wall behind them to keep her in place.

Pain radiated from the contact, driving home the point that this man was deadly serious.

She turned her head hard to the right, escaping the punishment of his mouth long enough to scream. Thank God her breath had come back to fill her lungs and give her the strength now to shriek with all the power that blessed oxygen provided.

Still, the welcome chance to scream came back for all of about two seconds, until he cold-cocked her in the temple.

Bloody bastard.

Jenny went reeling sideways against the wall, falling to the ground. He was on top of her in an instant, breathing hard and sweating, the stench of his fear and excitement making her stomach roil. His clammy hands pawed around her waist, lifting her dress despite her frantic, disoriented kicks. The blow to her head had robbed her of perception for a few desperate moments, causing her to lash out at empty air.

"—I want to take care of you," David snapped in fierce whispers while he whipped off his necktie and looped it around her head, across her mouth as a gag. He yanked the knot tight, pulling her hair so hard that tears sprang instantly to her eyes. "I want to be with you and I promise you'll be happy. Damn it, you know I'd never hurt you on purpose…"

He wasn't just a bloody bastard. He'd turned into a raving lunatic. An erotomaniac, if her thorough education in pop psychology proved correct. Someone who fixated on a stranger or friend or celebrity and thought that person was in love with them.

No. No. *No.*

This would *not* happen to her. Her mind raced twelve steps ahead of her sluggish body, still mixed-up from the blow to her head as David rattled on, spewing nonsense words about how they would be so good together. Warm liquid trickled along her cheek in a slow drip and she guessed he must have broken her skin but she was too busy concentrating on how to get away to worry about the injury just yet.

Fluorescent lights glared down at her along with David's angry eyes as he railed at her for not staying "faithful" to him. He shoved her body away from the top step leading down the next flight of stairs. Strangely, as scared as she was at the moment, some small part of her mind rejoiced she could think and process what was happening to her at all.

Her phobia had ruled her life for so long, giving her groundless fears to keep her tucked away safely at home, and yet now she was facing the worst fear of her life and she didn't let it paralyze her.

She stretched, reached for her bag even while she knew her bare butt now touched the disgusting, disease-ridden floor of a public stairwell as he worked himself into a frenzy about her not staying true to him when she'd been dating him before Devon. She'd scratch his eyes out if she could, but she wanted to retrieve her weapon first—a more powerful weapon than mere fingernails, especially since her head still spun with dizziness.

If all else failed and he got her pinned, she'd simply disassociate from herself from the waist down and use her wild imagination to fly somewhere else in her head. But damn it, she didn't think she'd be failing because her fingertip just connected with her fallen suitcase.

Yes.

Pride filled her at that small accomplishment. Her keys rested inside the front zippered compartment, and on that key ring was one of the De-Luxe catalog's top sellers. A small device that flicked open into a baton heavy enough to whack Brady into next year.

Then she'd use the other end of the baton that doubled as a whistle to call for help.

Jenny Moore—Enraged, Righteous Amazon on the Warpath.

Oh yeah, she liked that better.

"—we'll go someplace more private after this," David continued to talk as he unbuckled his pants, looking down at her with real craziness in his eyes that was ten times darker and more disturbing than anything she'd ever seen in her mother's gaze even on her mom's worst nights. "I'll take you to a quiet little island where we can be alone and you won't be afraid—"

Jenny tuned out his onslaught of words as she dug into the zippered pocket, praying he wouldn't take note of her movements. Her fingernail ripped off against the jagged teeth, but she felt her keys, knew she could grab them—

Her work was interrupted by a ringing sound echoing through the cavernous, empty stairwell. David's cell phone, she realized vaguely, but he snapped it off in midring.

It seemed foolish to hope someone had heard the phone if no one had heard her abbreviated scream earlier. Digging deeper into the pocket, she hooked her finger around the ring just as David positioned himself between her legs, his pants jammed down enough to expose himself. She could knee him in a minute, but for one more second she needed every inch of stretch her legs could give her if she wanted that weapon—

A crash sounded one flight above them, followed by a shout that made her heart sing.

"Jenny?"

Devon.

She grunted out a response from behind the necktie, so damn grateful to have help she didn't think to be scared for him, too. That is, until she saw David reach into his jacket and withdraw a length of shiny black metal.

No.

Her incomprehensible greeting turned into a panicked, muffled shout.

HORROR CLOGGED Devon's throat at the sight of Jenny lying at the edge of a steep staircase, her dress bunched up around her thighs, blood trickling down the side of her face. Her yellow thong was still in place, but if the bastard had forced her—

He couldn't think about that now or he'd lose his focus. Screw up what he had to do since she wasn't out of danger yet. He'd just let the anger propel him forward, use his instincts now that he'd finally acknowledged that emotions could play an effective part in his orderly life. Every squelched surge of dislike for Brady came roaring back to life now, bound up with a ferocious need to avenge Jenny and whatever hell she'd been through while Devon had been feeling sorry for himself in the lobby bar.

He was already flying down the stairs when he

heard her muffled cry. He'd almost reached the landing where David stood hunched over her when Devon spotted the gun.

Pointed haphazardly at Jenny, the weapon glinted in the glare of fluorescent lights while Brady stared up at Devon. The guy was sweating profusely, his forehead slick and shiny in the stark light bouncing off creamy walls.

"Stop right there, Baines." Brady's voice bounced off the bare walls, rasping a shrill note as if he tried to speak softly but couldn't hide his excitement.

The sick bastard.

Devon raised his hands, not wanting to give the guy any motive for pulling a trigger and not trusting Brady to play smart or fair.

"I'm stopping." He couldn't even imagine what the hell Brady was thinking to try and hurt Jenny. Devon wasn't sure what had happened here tonight already, but he knew she'd been through too much. "You're in charge, dude."

Devon wanted to go to Jenny, but she was moving with slow determination behind Brady, withdrawing some sort of metal object from her fallen suitcase.

A weapon?

"Damn right I'm the one in control," Brady shot back as he mopped his forehead with a wilted cotton shirtsleeve. "I might not have ever gotten so much as a nod of approval from the hard-ass old man for my efforts, but now that he's out of the way, his blowhard colleagues can recognize my worth."

His thumb caressed the top of the handgun barrel and Devon didn't even want to think about the guy's sweaty finger slipping on the clip of the sleek firearm with a silencer on the nose. He had to get Jenny away from this maniac before he started firing, but Devon didn't dare risk another glance in her direction for fear Brady would look her way, too.

If Jen had any kind of weapon to use on this guy, Devon planned to give her every opportunity to retrieve it.

"They voted me out so you could take over," Devon admitted, hoping to appease the ego-tripping lunatic by feeding him whatever the hell he wanted to hear. "You were smart to get close to Melinda Scott."

Brady snorted his disgust. "That's debatable. She's a crazy bitch. I never saw someone go off with their fists the way she did the other night."

Devon processed the words, but his eyes flicked to Jenny who nodded at him, her hidden weapon now fully extended into a nightstick that looked ready to do business. She held it with a steady hand, her gaze surprisingly calm and focused.

Just looking at her turned Devon's heart over in his chest. He'd never met a woman so fearless. So strong. This bold lady didn't hide from life. She made smart choices that worked for her, that made her happy. He'd been an idiot not to see that before.

"Melinda's been arrested, you know." Devon tensed, waiting for Jenny to make her move as he stretched the truth for David's sake. Roy's wife had only been picked up for questioning, after all. But maybe he'd see the benefit of turning himself in.

"For what?" David glanced back at Jenny, his hand twitching the gun he pointed at her.

Thank God Jenny had stashed her sleek metal club in the folds of the dress she'd yanked down to cover her knees. If only Devon could get the firearm off her for a moment, he would rush Brady in a heartbeat. But he needed a break, something that would distract the guy.

"I think you know what for." Devon decided to gamble with pissing him off since he didn't have a clue how to talk down a man holding a gun. Give him something mechanical over head games any day. But for Jenny's sake, he'd take a stab at playing shrink to get a rise out of her attacker. "The cops seemed interested in the time she spent in the hotel with you the other night. Something to do with a three-way gone awry?"

The trick worked all too well. Dave's eyebrows knitted together so hard a thick, blue vein popped out down the center of his forehead. Devon could practically see his heartbeat slamming through that pulsing, pissed-off blood vessel.

"She doesn't know what she's talking about." Dave waved the gun for emphasis, and that was all the opening Devon needed.

He charged him, tackling his arm to get control of the gun. A shot fired, blasting up into the ceiling with deceptive quiet thanks to the silencer on the barrel. The fluorescent light overhead went out, the plastic casing shattering, raining shards down on their heads as he pummeled Brady's hand into the floor to free the weapon.

Another shot blasted free before Devon jarred it loose, but Jenny must have known enough to stay out of the way. From a few feet behind him he heard a sharp whistle pierce the stairwell, scoring his eardrums.

A fire alarm?

Wrenching himself up off the floor and Brady, Devon cocked his arm back to throw a punch. And another.

Brady doubled over to protect his gut from the next blow Devon's fist would have delivered, but that didn't save the guy from the whack of a metal nightstick on his legs.

Devon turned to see Jenny behind him, her thin but effective baton in her raised hand. He would have gladly finished off Brady by himself, but after what she'd been through—he prayed it wasn't any worse than the cut on her head—she had the right to a piece of vengeance for herself.

The stairwell door burst open a floor below them and hotel security pounded up the steps, armed and shouting. Quintessence had bumped up safety measures after the beating in the hotel earlier that week, so the guards had guns drawn.

Devon backed away from Brady as the three officers surrounded them. Devon was only too glad to give over the crazy bastard to trained professionals because all he wanted right now was to see for himself if Jenny was okay. Untying the gag around her mouth with gentle hands, he gave the officers a quick explanation of finding Brady in the stairwell with her and the wrestling match for the gun that ensued.

He knew there'd be more questions and waiting around for police to arrive, but he needed to hold Jenny. Make sure she was okay. Before he could speak, she rushed to talk to him first.

"Thank you." Her words were raspy, her normally silky tones roughed up from a throat that had to be bone dry because of the gag.

He brushed her hair away from her face where pieces fell in disarray around her forehead, sticking in the stream of drying blood from her cut. The wound wasn't as deep as he'd feared, but he was careful not to touch her skin anywhere near the gash for fear of pulling it open again. The security guards multiplied around them as two-way radios crackled back and forth and curious hotel patrons nosed their way into doors on the floors above and below them.

"Thank me? Jesus, lady, I let you down in so many ways tonight." He couldn't even think about how easily he'd let her walk away from him earlier. A mistake he'd never repeat. "If I had insisted you go home, I would have been with you. I could have driven you—"

"You couldn't have made me leave and I would have resented you for pushing too hard if you'd tried." She pulled him up two steps, making way for a guard that arrived carrying handcuffs. "You were here when I needed you most even though I walked away before. Your timing—" her breath caught on a shaky note "—couldn't have been more perfect."

Fear for what she'd been through threatened to haul his knees right out from under him. She'd worked so hard to keep herself safe in the past. If David's delusional assault had destroyed her efforts to take a few risks... Devon couldn't think about it without a red rage descending on him.

"Are you okay?" He kept his voice steady, even. The last thing he wanted was to freak her out with anger on her behalf. She deserved better than that from him. "Did he hurt you anywhere besides your head?"

He was afraid to touch her, afraid to wrap her in his arms the way he wanted to in case she hid other injuries.

"I'm fine. He didn't—" she swallowed hard and straightened "—touch me. I'm not hurt anywhere else."

Not needing any other invitation, Devon folded her in his arms and held her tight, careful not to brush her face until a doctor could look at her cut. For now he just inhaled the faint scent of gardenia that clung to her clothes, her hair.

He didn't stop holding her until the police arrived, and even then he only managed to step away with an effort. He wasn't sure if her brush with danger had changed her mind about wanting to conquer her phobia or about her wish to walk away from him, but Devon knew her near miss had clarified a few things for him.

The right woman was worth waiting for and Jenny Moore was the woman he wanted—phobias and all. And as soon as he could get her alone, as soon as they'd given statements that would lock up crazy Dave Brady for a long time, Devon planned to tell Jenny how much he wanted her in his life.

15

SIX HOURS LATER, Jenny battled a bout of nerves as Devon walked her into her apartment in Seaside Heights. Not the kind of nerves she was accustomed to—her battle with Dave Brady had given her some perspective on her old fears. The nerves she experienced now were more about *The Talk* she sensed looming in her future with Devon.

But she could handle this now. She understood some fears were normal. Devon had helped her analyze her emotions instead of just reacting to them. She could separate the big fears from the smaller fears, weed out some of the emotional noise that didn't really matter.

She'd told him she'd be fine to return home on her own, but he'd insisted on driving her car for her, explaining that he could call for a cab to bring him back to Atlantic City and pick up his truck afterward.

She'd been too exhausted to argue at the time, but now that she opened the door to her place in the soft haze of early morning sunlight filtering through the clouds, Jenny wondered if she'd have enough strength to say goodbye to the coolest, most wonderful man she'd ever met. She watched him jog back down the stairs to her car to retrieve her trunk stuffed full of luxuries and regret pinched her heart.

The night had left her a little vulnerable, a little shaky. An EMT had bandaged the gash on her head after deciding she didn't need stitches, but the ordeal of the police questioning had rattled her.

Just hearing about the unholy alliance between Melinda Scott—an admitted nymphomaniac, according to a statement given by her devastated husband—and Dave Brady had left her queasy. The woman Melinda had beaten had regained consciousness late the night before, apparently. Her statement had helped police initiate the paperwork for David's arrest, but his assault on Jenny had speeded the process. Devon had also given the police the name of the waitress who'd tipped him off that David might be dangerous in case her statement was needed.

Between bouts of questioning and signing statements at the police station that night, Devon had explained to her that David's rift with the elder Brady had been wide, apparently leaving Dave adrift and prone to finding solace with women.

Sex.

And, eventually, a dangerous case of erotomania.

Melinda had been more into games of dominance and violence, and the two of them together seemed to bring out the worst in each other. Police had found two airline tickets to South America in David's possession after the arrest, along with the deed to some hole-in-the-wall property where he'd planned to take Jenny.

She shuddered at the thought of what might have happened.

Still, as uneasy as David made her, Jenny had walked out of Quintessence Hotel just before dawn with new confidence in herself and a feeling of resolve. She would start running her personal life with as much smooth efficiency as she conducted her professional relationships because she wasn't hiding behind some medical label anymore.

Like it or not, she was a woman full of contrasts and contradictions, and beginning today, she would embrace the good and the bad in her personal inventory. She would continue to battle her agoraphobia, but she wouldn't fear it anymore. She'd seen into the eyes of a genuinely crazy person and she knew more now than ever that *she* wasn't one of them.

"You sure you don't want some takeout?" Devon offered again as he lugged her trunk full of belongings—her comfort items—into her apartment. He'd already asked if she was hungry on the ride over but she'd been too preoccupied to eat. "A breakfast sandwich? Coffee?"

"No, thanks." She peered around her home with new eyes. Wiser eyes. Taking in the rows of scented candles on her dining room table, the piles of antique, leather bound books spilling out from her shelves and the starched antique linens covering her tables and dressers, Jenny acknowledged that it was no wonder she never wanted to leave her house. She'd made a sumptuous retreat here, a feast for the senses with pretty surroundings and a wealth of ways to stay entertained.

No more beating herself up about it if she chose to grill fresh veggies on her back patio for dinner instead of forcing herself to mingle with the crush of suscreen-slathered tourists on the boardwalk to eat a hot dog crammed with everything except for real nutrients.

When her business day was done, she simply liked her privacy. No harm, no foul. Her home was her choice, not a prison.

"I know you must be tired." Devon stalked closer, his tall, darkly handsome good looks only intensified by his rumpled dress shirt open at the collar. "But I need to talk to you—to tell you a few things before I take off. I called for a cab when I went downstairs for your trunk. The car should be here soon."

She appreciated his thoughtfulness even as she realized there would be no chance to drag him into her bed one last time. It wouldn't have been fair to him anyway, but it would have been…nice.

More than nice.

She didn't know how she'd ever say goodbye to him. To the best week of sleepless nights she'd ever experienced.

"I've been meaning to talk to you, too. I know I

haven't been fair about shutting things down with us, but I want you to know I'm doing my best. I just need to fix… No, that's not true." She was done fixing herself. She'd stretch her boundaries maybe. Get out a little more. But she was strong and happy with her life already. "I just want to try living the things I've learned this week, implement a new approach to my phobia, before I could give any relationship a fair shot."

The notion of being without him hurt, though, and no matter how much pleasure she took from her familiar surroundings, her old painted furniture mixed with extravagant chandeliers, Jenny couldn't escape that ache.

"I don't expect anything from you, Jen, other than for you to believe me when I say I'm crazy about you and that I want a shot with you whenever you're ready." He paused a few inches from her in the middle of the living room floor, hand trailing over the back of her sofa's bleached slipcover as he gave her space to absorb what he was saying.

He'd do that for her? She couldn't even scavenge up words to tell him how much that meant.

"And if that's not what you want," he continued, his plan all thought out even if he was offering her options, "I'll hate it and it will hurt like hell, but I'll respect your wishes because you're one incredible lady and you deserve whatever you want in life. In love."

She blinked. Tried to let his words to sink in. He wasn't making some over the top declaration. He was simply leaving the door open for a future and giving her room to think about the idea.

"You'd wait for me?" She wrapped her arms around herself, not having gotten rid of the chill that pervaded ever since David Brady had appeared on the stairwell to scare the living daylights out of her.

"Definitely. I know you're not ready for a bigger commitment yet, and that this thing between us came on strong and fast." He scratched his head. "Hell, Jen, I've never seen anything like it, but I know it's too good to let go just because you need more time. It just so happens, I've got time to spare."

He would wait.

The possibilities unrolled in her mind, shining in front of her with the promise of something amazing, something that could really last. She stepped closer, reached out to touch him and make the dream real.

"You know, I don't think I really recognized how much stronger I could be if I got control of my fears, but tonight I realized that whatever that maniac had in store for me—I wasn't powerless. I'm smart and quick-witted. And while my phobia has never been rational, I think I gained some more perspective on it to help me talk myself out of my fears next time I hyperventilate around a stranger."

She'd talked herself through the encounter with David. Did what she had to do. Maybe she could find ways to brave a future with Devon if he was willing to try. He had so many reasons to push her away, and yet he kept making an effort.

"Did you hyperventilate tonight?" He stared down at her, his forehead creased with concern. "I hadn't even thought about how that could incapacitate you."

"It was close." Those first moments of screaming silence were terrifying. "There was a second when I couldn't catch my breath, but I've faced that sensation so many times this week that I was able to think my way past it. You gave me that ability."

He shook his head, refusing to take credit. "No. You've been the one taking all the chances from the start. I'm just glad to be along for the ride."

He gathered up her hands, warming them between his and reminding her how good it could be to have someone around to chase away the chills, to cheer her on when she took chances instead of racing her to the doctor or a shrink the way her mother always had.

"But you know the ride isn't over yet, don't you?" She wanted to be certain he knew what he was getting himself into if he opted to stick around and try to make this work. No doubt there would be plenty of ups and downs as she found her footing. "I've still got a long way to grow."

Devon lifted the back of her hand to his mouth and brushed light kisses along the ridge of her knuckles, dipping in the valleys between.

"A roller coaster ride that doesn't end? Dating you sounds like my idea of heaven."

Her heart warmed as emotions she dared not name flowed through her. *Dating*. An easy commitment she could make. They could take things slow. Go out to the movies at midnight. Maybe a less populated matinee. Nice, normal ways to spend time together.

Normal sounded like *her* idea of heaven.

She could make a few changes around her place to help him be more comfortable here when he spent the night. Maybe open the space up a little more. Perhaps she could put in a whole new row of windows to let in light. Life. She'd never want Devon to feel closed in here for even a moment.

Desire for him tingled her insides at the same time as a surge of tenderness and caring threatened to put happy tears in her eyes.

"Isn't it amazing how instant attraction could turn into something so much deeper?" She never would have guessed the delectable stranger who strode into her hotel room would turn out to be a man who could offer her so much more than sizzling sex.

Or that nurturing a relationship, caring about another person brought a feeling of safety all its own.

"Science suggests that our brains are actually well equipped to make complex decisions in a fraction of a second, taking into account vast amounts of stored knowledge on many different levels." He wrapped her arms around his neck and then slid his hands about her waist to draw her near.

Making her *very* aware of him and how much he wanted her.

"I didn't know that there was much science involved that first night you seduced me right out of my clothes."

"But isn't it comforting to know there are rational reasons behind love at first sight?"

Jenny's heart skipped a beat and for a moment she wondered if she'd hyperventilate at Devon's mention of the *L* word for the second time in this conversation. But no, maybe that breathless clench of her heart had more to do with wild joy than old, misplaced fears.

"You think so?"

"I know so. And I'm going to give you all the time in the world to come around to my way of thinking." Slanting his mouth over hers he kissed her, tasting her lips with slow deliberation like a man who had no intention of rushing her.

Savoring the contact, Jenny molded her body to his, ready for more. Hungry for more. Wouldn't Devon be surprised if she ended up being the one who nudged their relationship forward faster? This kind of kiss made her realize there would be a lot of delectable benefits to getting her life together sooner rather than later.

When he broke away she had to blink her way back to their conversation, her thoughts clouded by steam heat and want of Devon. What had they been talking about?

Oh yeah.

Love at first sight.

"I'm pretty well convinced already," she admitted, looking forward to getting to know Devon much, much better. "I have the feeling I'm going to really like dating."

"And the good news is that we're already past the first three dates, so now it's nothing but wine and roses."

"Who cares about wine and roses? I'm in it for your body, Baines. Get used to it."

"Do with me what you will, lady. I'm just so damn grateful you're safe. That you're willing to give us a chance." He dropped kisses on the top of her head and squeezed her hard.

"Do you have to go back to Wildwood today? Or are you going back to the Philadelphia house?" His cab would be here soon and they'd have to wait to talk another day.

Jenny appreciated that he wanted to give their relationship a try, but she still didn't know how they'd work out the logistics. She tucked closer to his chest, her ear settled on his shoulder since she wasn't sure she wanted to see his face when he told her his plans.

"I'm going to be in Philly a lot the next month while I put my house on the market."

Her head wrenched up to meet his gaze.

"You're moving?"

"I'm thinking about getting a place closer to the shore. Farther up the coast than Wildwood. Maybe open a new branch of the engineering firm." He shrugged. Smiled. "The Garden State is growing on me."

"Are you sure?" She could hardly believe he would make such a big move before she had a chance to get her life in order, but it would make dating easier. More frequent. All the more wonderful. "Because I could make a few trips to Philly if I had the incentive of sensual adventure waiting for me on the other end of the interstate."

"You'd do that for me?"

"In a minute. I don't want you to think you need to do all the changing for me. I'm ready for some changes, too." She'd knocked down all kinds of personal barriers this week and it felt—incredible. "I bet I'd like Philadelphia with all the historical significance and the great music. Besides, I hear there are a lot of crazies in Jersey."

"Then I'll fit right in since I think I'm developing a bit of an obsession for a local woman." Sliding his arm around her waist, he guided her over to the living room window so he could peer out over the rows of short apartment buildings and local businesses between her place and the boardwalk. "Maybe you could give me some pointers for coming to terms with it. It's getting so bad I don't even need a two-hundred-foot drop to jump-start my heart anymore. Just seeing you provides a major jolt."

Smiling, she could easily imagine herself walking

the streets of her neighborhood with Devon by her side to distract her.

Kiss her.

Tempt her beyond reason.

"That sounds like a beneficial disorder to me. I vote you indulge your obsession as soon as possible if you're really intent on moving. And if you happen to need anywhere to sleep over while you're house hunting, I know of a really great apartment with all sorts of luxurious indulgences."

Maybe helping him house hunt would give her an excuse to explore more neighborhood terrain. And if nothing else, it gave her a good reason to invite him to stay with her now and then. She spied his cab pulling up to the curb below but noticed he wasn't exactly sprinting to go meet his ride.

"I'll bet you throw a hell of a sleepover party."

"Did I mention I have a lot more lingerie in my personal collection of indulgences?" She wasn't above throwing a little sexual enticement into the mix if it would make him wave his cab away.

Growling in his throat he turned her to face him, to face her future with him.

"No more mentions of lingerie if you still want me to take things slow for a while." His dark eyes glittered with heat she couldn't wait to explore, his gaze not wavering even when the cab below laid on the horn. "That's an off-limits discussion for your own protection."

"Your powers of persuasion are making me suspect I'll be able to get my act together sooner than you think." She sketched a touch up his chest to trace a circle around his heart. "And you're invited for a sleepover anytime you like. Starting tonight if you opt to go downstairs and tell the cab driver you've changed your mind about leaving."

"Yeah? I'll run down and give him a fat tip for his trouble if you're sure." He pulled out his phone, as if to tell the driver to wait another minute.

Arching on her toes to finish the kiss he'd started earlier, Jenny claimed Devon for her own with a mating of mouths he wouldn't forget. She didn't know exactly what their future held, but she knew this wasn't a man to make decisions lightly, no matter what he spouted about the brain's ability to process huge amounts of stored data in an instant.

If he wanted to move to New Jersey permanently and be near her, he had more than sex on his mind. He wanted to make things work between them as badly as she did even though she'd been afraid to hope. She couldn't wait to explore the rest of her feelings for Devon, but for right now, she already knew one thing for sure.

Breaking their kiss, she peered up at him in the soft morning light filtering in through the window as they stood together where anyone passing by on the street could look up and see them.

"I'm sure. And about that notion of love at first

sight?" Smiling, she traced his lips with one finger. "I don't need any scientific evidence. I'm already a believer."

* * * * *

Look for Joanne Rock's next book
from Harlequin Blaze
Part of the PERFECT TIMING *miniseries*
Coming in June 2006

If you enjoyed what you just read,
then we've got an offer you can't resist!

Take 2 bestselling love stories FREE!

Plus get a FREE surprise gift!

AFTER HOURS
At this trendy salon, the fun begins when the lights go down

It's the trendiest salon in Miami...
and landlord Troy Barrington is determined
to shut it down. As part owner and massage
therapist, Peggy Underwood can't let him—
and his ego—win. So she'll use all of the
sensual, er, spa tools at her disposal to
change his mind.

MIDNIGHT OIL
by Karen Kendall
On sale April 2006

HARLEQUIN®

Blaze™

COMING NEXT MONTH

#243 OBSESSION Tori Carrington
Dangerous Liaisons, Bk. 2
Anything can happen in the Quarter.... Hotel owner Josie Villefranche knows that better than most. Ever since a woman was murdered in her establishment, business has drastically declined. She's very tempted to allow sexy Drew Morrison to help her take her mind off her troubles—until she learns he wants much more than just a night in her bed....

#244 WHAT HAVE I DONE FOR ME LATELY? Isabel Sharpe
It's All About Attitude
Jenny Hartmann's sizzling bestseller *What Have I Done for Me Lately?* is causing an uproar across the country. And now Jenny's about to take her own advice—by having a sexual fling with Ryan Masterson. What Jenny isn't prepared for is that the former bad boy is good in bed—and even better at reading between the lines!

#245 SHARE THE DARKNESS Jill Monroe
FBI agent Ward Cassidy thinks Hannah Garret is a criminal. And Hannah suspects Ward is working for her ex-fiancé, the man who now wants her dead. But when Hannah and Ward get caught for hours in a hot, darkened elevator, the sensual pull of their bodies tells them all they *really* need to know....

#246 MIDNIGHT OIL Karen Kendall
After Hours, Bk. 1
It's the trendiest salon in Miami...and landlord Troy Barrington is determined to shut it down. As part owner and massage therapist, Peggy Underwood can't let him—and his ego—win. So she'll use all of the sensual, er, *spa* tools at her disposal to change his mind.

#247 AFTERNOON DELIGHT Mia Zachary
Rei Davis is a tough-minded judge who wishes someone could see her softer side. Chris London is a lighthearted matchmaker who wishes someone would take him seriously. When Rei walks into Lunch Meetings, the dating service Chris owns, and the computer determines that they're a perfect match, sparks fly! But will all their wishes come true?

#248 INTO TEMPTATION Jeanie London
The White Star, Bk. 4
It's the sexiest game of cat and mouse she's ever played. MI6 agent Lindy Gardner is determined to capture Joshua Benedict—and the stolen amulet in his possession. The man is leading her on a sensual chase across two continents that will only make his surrender oh, so satisfying.

www.eHarlequin.com